A Thousand Shades of Blue

A Thousand Shades of Blue

Robin Stevenson

ORCA BOOK PUBLISHERS

Library and Archives Canada Cataloguing in Publication

Stevenson, Robin H. (Robin Hjørdis), 1968-
A thousand shades of blue / written by Robin Stevenson.

ISBN 978-1-55143-921-1

I. Title.

PS8637.T487T48 2008   jC813'.6   C2008-903050-8

First published in the United States, 2008
Library of Congress Control Number: 2008928575

Summary: A yearlong sailing trip to the Bahamas reveals deep wounds in Rachel's family and brings out the worst in Rachel.

Orca Book Publishers gratefully acknowledges the support for its publishing programs provided by the following agencies: the Government of Canada through the Book Publishing Industry Development Program and the Canada Council for the Arts, and the Province of British Columbia through the BC Arts Council and the Book Publishing Tax Credit.

Design by Teresa Bubela
Cover artwork by Janice Kun
Author photo by David Lowes

ORCA BOOK PUBLISHERS
PO Box 5626, STN. B
VICTORIA, BC CANADA
V8R 6S4

ORCA BOOK PUBLISHERS
PO Box 468
CUSTER, WA USA
98240-0468

www.orcabook.com
Printed and bound in Canada.
Printed on 100% PCW recycled paper.
11 10 09 08 • 4 3 2 1

To Cheryl May, for all the memories of a magical year
aboard the sailboat Tara.

Acknowledgments

Many thanks to Ilse and Giles Stevenson for their support and encouragement; to Pat Schmatz for her careful reading and insightful suggestions; to the fiction critique group of the Victoria Writer's Society for providing helpful feedback on the early chapters; and to Sarah Harvey for her thoughtful and astute advice.

One

Sailing in the Bahamas is a dream come true, right? Clear blue water, suntanning every day, cocktails on the deck with ice cubes clinking, tropical fish, brightly colored coral reefs.

Here's the reality: That clear blue water never stops moving. The boat doesn't always rock you gently. Sometimes it throws you around so violently you'd sell your soul to get to shore. More often it just drives you crazy with its constant motion and keeps you slightly off balance. The sun burns your skin. The refrigeration breaks down, and there are no ice cubes. Everything tastes salty: your hair, your lips, the tips of your fingers. The coral reefs are fragile and damaged, and the fish that swim over them can carry ciguatera, a toxin which damages your nervous system so that heat feels like ice and cold burns like fire.

Nothing is what it seems. Nothing.

I'm sitting on the foredeck of our sailboat. This is what passes for privacy now. My parents and my younger brother, Tim, are twenty feet behind me. They can see me if they stand up, but at least I can't hear them over the sound of the waves breaking against the hull and the wind luffing the badly trimmed jib. Sailing only looks quiet and peaceful when you're watching from the shore. I lie down, close my eyes against the sun and try not to think about what happened back in Georgetown. After all, we've left. We've sailed away. Georgetown, the small Bahamian community and cruising hub, is behind us now.

"Rachel," Dad yells. "We could use a little help back here."

You'd think between the three of them, they could manage. I stand up and make my way back to the cockpit, holding on to the rigging as the boat rises and falls beneath me. The wind has picked up, and it's getting a little rough out here.

I sit down on the bench beside my brother. "What's up?"

Mom is at the helm, standing with her hands gripping the big wheel. Dad is frowning at the chart.

"Change of plans," he says. "Calabash Bay isn't going to be safe with the winds shifting to the west. We're going to go in here instead."

I scan the low barren shoreline of Long Island. "In where?" All I can see is rocks.

Dad stabs at the chart with his finger. "Joe Sound."

Tim reads aloud from the guidebook. "*A very protected anchorage with a narrow entrance channel.*"

"No shit," I say, staring at the rocks. "So narrow we can't see it. Are you sure we're in the right spot?"

Dad nods. "Absolutely."

"Right there," Mom says suddenly, pointing. "God, it's really narrow. Mitch, are you sure this is the best plan?"

"Unless anyone else has a better idea, or feels like sailing all night," Dad says. "It'll be dark in a couple of hours."

Tim and I drop the sails and tie them down quickly. As we get closer to shore, the channel looks even narrower. The waves behind us push us forward, and the water changes from blue to green: It's getting shallower.

"I don't like the look of this at all," Mom says.

"Let's not have negative attitudes." Dad glances down at the chart again. "It should be perfectly straightforward."

"Perhaps you'd like to take the helm then." Her voice is tight and brittle.

He takes the wheel from her without saying anything.

Tim picks up the guidebook again. "*The channel is six feet deep at its center. Follow the imaginary line into the calm waters of Joe Sound.*" He snorts. "Follow the imaginary line?"

"Get up on the foredeck, you two. Guide us in." Dad's voice is tense.

Tim and I go and stand at the bow, gripping the fore-stay tightly. I try to find the bluest, deepest water and signal to Dad. It's not as easy as it sounds. There are a thousand shades of blue. Anyone can tell the difference between water that's two feet deep and water that's ten feet deep, but trying to tell the difference between the subtle shades of turquoise that differentiate four feet and six feet is a bit more difficult.

And yet essential. Our boat needs five feet of water to stay afloat.

"A little more to starboard," I yell, pointing.

Tim is shaking his head. "This is crazy. There isn't enough water."

Once we're in the channel, there'll be no way to turn around. The rocks on either side of the channel are jagged and sharp, and I can't help agreeing with Tim: This is crazy.

Dad is coming to the same conclusion. "It's too narrow," he shouts. "I'm turning back." The bow of the boat starts to swing back to port.

I look down through the water and see the yellowish sheet of rock on the bottom. "It's too late to turn," I yell. "It's too shallow."

There's an awful crunch, and the boat stops dead. My forehead smashes into the bow rail, and Tim grabs me to keep me from falling overboard. Then there's another awful crunch, and another. The waves are lifting us up and flinging us back down onto the rocks. The whole boat shudders horribly with each impact.

Dad throws the engine into reverse. It roars, and we lift and crash and then somehow, just as suddenly, we're free and floating again. I point wildly to starboard. Dad puts *Shared Dreams* into forward, the boat swings back into the channel, and we slip through into the still blue water beyond. It looks like a wide shallow lake: acres of pale blue water surrounded by beach and scrub and low hills.

We set the anchor. I rub my forehead; a tender bump is starting to form where I whacked it on the rail. I figure everyone must be shaken by what happened, but no one says anything about it. Dad's pretty quiet. I bet he's furious with himself. Mom and Tim stow the genoa and tie the cover on the main sail, and Dad jumps in the water to make sure the bottom of the boat is okay.

As for me, I'm starving. It's my turn to cook—we have a schedule for absolutely everything. I'm stirring noodles into boiling water when Dad climbs back on board and stands dripping in the cockpit.

"Bad news, folks," he says. "The rudder's pretty badly cracked. No way we can fix that without getting the boat hauled out of the water. And there's no marina here. We'll have to sail it back to Georgetown." He shrugs, like it's not such a big deal. Like it's not the end of the fucking world.

A dull pain thuds in my chest. Tim and I stare at each other. The water in my pot starts to boil over, and I pull it off the burner, slopping scalding hot water and noodles down the side of my hand. I swear under my breath. It hurts, but at least it's a distraction.

Tim chews on the edge of his finger. "Isn't there some way we can fix it here?"

"No, it's a big job." Dad rubs his chin. "I'll slap some underwater epoxy on tonight to help it hold together for the sail back. We'll head to Georgetown in the morning."

I want to scream at him. I want to tell him that Georgetown is absolutely the last place we should go.

He has no idea that this stupid crack in the rudder could destroy our already messed-up family. And I can't tell him without destroying it myself.

Two

The reason we were in the Bahamas in the first place was, according to my parents, to spend quality time together as a family. Don't laugh. Although, why not? Four people who could barely stand each other on a good day moving onto a small boat together? I would have laughed if it wasn't my life that was getting turned upside down.

When Dad first made the big announcement about dragging us off on this sailing trip, it all seemed totally unreal to me. That was four months ago, but if there is one thing I've learned, it's that the past matters. Tim's the history buff, not me, but even I know that you can't make sense of the present without understanding the past. So here's how it all went down.

We were all sitting around the dinner table, back in our four-bedroom house in Hamilton. After my sister Emma moved out, Mom and Dad decided that Dinner Time Was Family Time. So there we were like some TV sitcom family, eating meatloaf, asking each other polite questions about our days and pretending we cared.

I was kind of nervous that night because I'd dyed my hair a bit. I'd added a blue streak, which wasn't as dramatic as it sounds. My hair is dyed black anyway, and at that time it was a spiky mess of half-dreads that didn't quite work out. So the blue wasn't actually as noticeable as I'd hoped. Still, I was waiting for Dad to freak out.

He didn't even notice.

I poured ketchup on my meatloaf and mushed it up. Roadkill. I pushed it around my plate.

"So," Dad said, "your mother and I have been talking, and we've got some news to share."

I couldn't help glancing at Tim. He was gripping the edge of the table, his skinny face white as the walls. I knew exactly what he was thinking.

D-I-V-O-R-C-E.

A part of me actually felt relieved. Like maybe we could all just get it over with. Then I looked at Dad. He had a big grin on his face.

"We've decided we're going to take a family trip," he said.

It took a minute for the words to sink in. Okay. Not a divorce then. "I hate to break it to you, Dad," I said, "but we're a little old for Disneyland."

He ignored my sarcasm. "This is a lot better than Disneyland, Rach. We're going to sail our boat down to the Bahamas."

This was something Dad had always talked about doing someday—like, after Tim and I are gone, and he retires. We hadn't done all that much sailing as a family.

I'd never been interested. Sailing back and forth in Hamilton harbor, with the steel factories belching out smoke in the background, is not all that exciting. Our biggest trip ever had been an eight-hour sail to Toronto: slogging through the rain with the engine on all day, fish and chips at the marina restaurant for dinner, sleeping with the boat tied to a wobbly finger slip with the mosquitoes biting and the gas dock-lights beaming in through our windows all night long. I looked at Mom. "He's kidding, right?"

She'd been out running, and her hair was still all wet from the rain. She tucked it behind her ears and shook her head. "We thought it'd be good for us all. For our family."

Tim was smiling uncertainly, his eyes flicking back and forth between Mom, Dad and me as if he was trying to figure out what was going on, or waiting for clues so he'd know how to react.

Dad leaned toward me. "What do you think, Rachel? Sounds like fun, don't you think?"

I lifted my chin and looked right at him. I couldn't think of anything I wanted to do less than spend god knows how long trapped on a thirty-six-foot sailboat with my family. "Oh yeah, Dad."

He looked at me uncertainly. I almost laughed. He wasn't sure whether I was being serious or sarcastic. Well, Dad, that's what you get for spending all your time at the office fixing other people's messed-up kids.

"Sounds like a riot," I said. "I look forward to hearing all about it when you get back."

He leaned back and pushed his chair away from the table. "You're coming with us."

"I'll stay with Jen. Her parents won't mind."

"The point of this trip is for us to spend time together," he said firmly. "As a family."

I snorted.

Dad looked bewildered. "What?"

No one said anything. Tim looked at me anxiously and shook his head ever so slightly.

I ignored him. "Spending time with us isn't usually high on your list of priorities, Dad."

He hesitated, rubbed his chin and looked at Mom for help.

She just shrugged. "Rach, you've hardly touched your meatloaf."

I stared at the mess on my plate. "I'm not hungry."

Dad cleared his throat. "This family is very important to me," he said. "You are all very important to me."

He looked kind of sad, but none of us said anything. Dad's big on teenagers expressing their feelings, but only in his office. In our house, the rules are a little different: If you can't say something nice, don't say anything at all.

Most of the time, no one says anything at all.

"How would we get to the Bahamas from here?" Tim asked.

He was always trying to smooth things over, but it was still a good question. We kept our boat on Lake Ontario, and even I knew that the lake was nowhere near the ocean.

"There's a series of canals," Dad said. He was starting to smile again. "Wait, I'll get the chart and show you." He stood up. "Be right back."

I waited until he'd left the room. "Male bonding? You and Dad are going to be the navigators, are you?"

"I just wanted to know how we'd get there," Tim said.

I narrowed my eyes at him. "You're such a loser, Tim. Always kissing up to Dad."

Mom stood up and smoothed her track pants over her thighs. "That's enough, Rachel."

"May I be excused?" I asked.

"Just wait. Your dad really wants to show you the charts. He's so excited about this."

"What about you? Are you excited? Or is it all about Dad, as usual?"

"Rachel…" Mom made a funny little gesture with her hands, lifting them up and dropping them again like it was all too much. Too heavy. She's skinny like me but almost a foot taller. Seriously. I'm five foot nothing. Usually she looks really healthy in an athletic, outdoorsy way, but that night she looked really tired.

Tim gave me a dirty look. He hates it when anyone fights. He'd rather pretend that we really are that happy sit-com family.

I stood up to leave, but Dad came back in before I could make my escape.

"Sit down," he said. "I want to show you this."

Tim looked at me pleadingly. I felt like a shit for calling him a loser, so I sat back down.

"Here," Dad said, pushing plates aside to make room on the table for the big chart book. "We sail to Oswego; then we take the mast down and enter the Erie Canals." His index finger skipped across the chart, tracing a thin, blue, snaking line. "Here, there's a whole series of locks we go through, right to the Hudson River. We put the mast back up here, at Castleton-on-Hudson, and...right down the river to New York Harbor."

I'd never left Ontario, except for a couple of vacations in Florida and one trip to the Calgary Stampede when I was seven.

"And then—into the Atlantic?" Tim asked.

"You got it." Dad glanced at Mom. "Well, actually there is an inland waterway. The ICW—Intra-Coastal Waterway, it's called."

Mom leaned forward, her elbows on the table. "It's a bunch of connected rivers and canals and lakes that goes all the way down to Florida. So we don't actually have to do much sailing on the open ocean at all."

"We want to cross over to the Bahamas by early December." Dad had a big grin on his face. He didn't seem to have noticed that neither Tim nor I was jumping up and down with excitement.

Tim started to pick at his fingernails. "How long would we be gone for?" he asked.

Dad cleared his throat. "About a year."

I just sat and stared at him. Then I turned to Mom. "What about school? I can't miss a whole year." I couldn't get my head around this at all. A year away from Jen and all my friends? A year stuck on a boat with my family?

"You and Tim can do your courses by correspondence," Mom said. "We'll arrange everything before we go."

"My family spent a year in New Zealand when I was sixteen," Dad says. "I didn't want to go, but you know what? It was one of the best things my parents ever did for me."

I stared at them both. "You can't be serious. There is no way I'm doing this."

Mom ignored me. "It'll be nice for us all to have more time together," she said.

That's my mom—denial in action. I swear, sometimes I think she's living on a different planet.

Three

The thing that upset me most about the whole trip idea was the pretense that somehow they were doing this for us. For our family. As if a family is something other than the people who make it up. As if it could be good for the family to do something that half the people in the family didn't want to do. Okay, Mom hadn't admitted that she didn't want to, but she'd never liked sailing much. She always got seasick. And Tim was so desperate to believe that we were a happy family that he'd have gone along with anything. But I definitely didn't want to go.

As for Emma? Well, of course no one had even bothered to ask her what she thought. When I brought up the subject with my parents, they didn't say anything. They just looked at each other, all uneasy and dishonest.

"What?" I asked, suddenly feeling anxious. Tim was watching me, his green eyes half-hidden by his glasses and his floppy hair.

Mom put down her coffee mug. "Honey, Emma's not coming with us."

I stared at them both. "You're kidding me, right?"

"It'd be hard for her," Mom said. "Unsettling."

I pictured Emma's wide blue eyes, her goofy pink-gummed smile and slightly crooked teeth. She'd been doing great lately. But I had a head full of jagged memories: Emma banging her head against the bedroom wall, Emma biting her fingers until they bled, Emma ripping up my best sketches because I wouldn't let her use my new charcoal pencils. I pushed the memories aside.

"Did you even ask her? Did anyone even bother to ask her if she'd like to come?"

The answer was obvious in the way they exchanged glances.

"This whole thing about doing a trip for the family is a load of crap if part of the family isn't even included." I stood up. The sunlight was streaming in, and Mom, Dad and Tim were dark silhouettes against the kitchen window. "Count. Me. Out."

I didn't want to go anyway. A few weeks, maybe. A whole freaking year? Missing all of grade eleven, leaving my friends, being stuck with my parents and Tim the Nerd? No thank you. And leaving Emma for that long?

I couldn't even believe they were considering it.

It had been less than a year since Emma moved out. I always visited her after school on Tuesdays. Tuesday was our special day.

The Tuesday after Mom and Dad told us about the sailing trip, I told Mom I didn't want to go to the group home. I knew about the trip and Emma didn't, and I couldn't stand the thought of lying to her.

Mom was making coffee, still in her housecoat. She was quiet for a moment; then she put on her reasonable voice. You know when parents get that reasonable voice going that they are about to say something that isn't really reasonable at all.

"Rach, there's no point in telling her yet. She'll just get upset."

"Maybe if it's so upsetting for her, we shouldn't be doing it. Did you think about that, Mom? That maybe if you feel you have to lie about it, you might be doing something wrong?"

She looked away from me and brushed at some coffee grounds on the counter. "If we tell her about the trip now, she'll be upset right up until we leave."

"Yeah, then you'd have to deal with it." I leaned my elbows on the table. "Much better to spring it on her at the last minute and let the staff deal with her being totally freaked out when no one visits for a year."

"It won't be a whole year," Mom protested. "I'll fly home to see her at least twice."

"I'm sure that'll take care of everything," I said. "Two visits in a year. She'll just be getting used to being abandoned, and then you'll come back for a few days and do it all over again."

She didn't say anything for a minute. Her mouth was

a hard thin line. Finally she put both hands flat on the counter and without even looking at me, she said, "We're doing this for you, you know. You and Tim, but mostly you."

I pushed my chair away from the table, its legs screeching against the gray linoleum. "Don't give me that."

"I'm serious, Rachel." She hesitated. "We're worried about you."

"We? We? You and who else?"

"Your father and I."

"Right." I snorted. "Well, if you're so concerned about me, you can do me a favor and forget the whole idea."

She went quiet again. Her hair was all sticking up on one side, dirty blond bed head, the same color mine would be if I didn't dye it. She kept trying to smooth it down, patting it like it was an animal curled up on her head. Finally she gave a long sigh. "You seem so angry all the time. Since Emma left...I don't know. I can't talk to you anymore. I thought, maybe, if we had more time together..."

I swallowed hard. Mom had no idea why I'd had such a crappy year, and I sure as shit wasn't going to tell her. I stood up. "So hold me hostage on the boat for a year. That should help." As I walked out the door, I turned and fired one last shot. "And don't try to make it my fault that you're abandoning Emma. You've probably wanted to do that for years."

As soon as the words came out of my mouth, I wanted to snatch them back. Mom looked like I'd slapped her.

Besides, Mom would have taken care of Emma forever. Dad was the one who had pushed for her to move out.

"It's developmentally appropriate for children to move out when they reach young adulthood," he used to argue.

Never mind that Emma hadn't done anything developmentally appropriate since the accident.

Mom would shake her head. "I don't think she's ready. I don't want her to feel like she's a failure if it doesn't work out."

"Failure is a stepping-stone to success," Dad would say.

That's Dad—the King of Clichés. I agreed with him though, for once. Not so much for Emma's sake as for the rest of us. Emma couldn't be left alone in the house, not even for five minutes. She does stuff without thinking, on impulse, and has no judgement about what's a good idea or what's safe. She has seizures too, even with all the meds she's on. And when she doesn't get her way, she gets pretty out of control. Disinhibition, the doctors call it. We just call it Emma's temper.

One time, when I was maybe twelve or so, I was screaming at her because she'd had this mammoth fit of rage and broken something of mine—I don't even remember what now. She broke a lot of stuff. Anyway, Dad pulled me aside and told me to get a grip. A few days later, he took me to see a social worker at the hospital. She tried to explain some stuff about head injuries to me and even showed me the CT scans of Emma's brain. You could see this black area where bleeding had basically destroyed part of her frontal lobe.

So I got that it wasn't her fault. But understanding that didn't make her any easier to deal with, and as we got older, I had to look after her more and more often. When Mom and Dad made the decision about her moving out, I was sad, sort of, but I was relieved too. I know how selfish that sounds, but that's how I felt.

I just wanted a more normal life.

Mom tried to act like she was in agreement with Dad's plan: My parents have always been big on presenting a united front in between the fights. But when Em left, Mom kind of fell apart. She sort of stopped talking, and Dad started spending even more time at his office.

So much for my dream of a normal life.

I ended up going to see Emma that night anyway. She had a big calendar in her room, to help her keep track of what was happening every day. On every Tuesday it said *RAE-RAE* in big green letters. She always bragged to the staff, telling them every week that her little sister was coming to see her. It wasn't easy to let someone like that down.

Though Mom and Dad didn't seem to be having any trouble with it.

Emma was waiting near the front door. "Rae-Rae!" She threw her arms around me and squished her face into my shoulder.

"Hey, Em." I grinned at her. She'd had a haircut—someone had given her bangs and cut her long hair to just above the shoulders. Mom would flip. She hated it when the staff made any decisions without consulting her. "Nice hairdo," I told her.

She touched her hair self-consciously. "Kelly did it."

"Looks good. So, what have you been doing? Were you working today?" Emma goes to a sheltered workshop where they make weird-looking teddy bears that get sold to raise money for the hospital.

"No, I'm sick," she said.

She didn't look sick. Sometimes she just doesn't want to go, and the staff don't push it too much.

"Come see what I made," Emma said. She tugged on my arm, pulled me down the hall into her room and pointed at a painting pinned to her wall.

"It's beautiful. Really great." I looked past the orange and blue swirls to the photo collage I'd made her when she moved out: old pictures of the three of us as little kids, of Dad looking young with a mustache and blue jeans, of Mom in short skirts and sunglasses. Those pictures reminded me of what I'd figured out about Emma's accident. It was the main reason I'd had such a crap year, but I hadn't told anyone.

I didn't even want to think about it.

The group home's glossy white paint was all scuffed up from the bumps of wheelchairs through narrow door frames. Schedules and medication charts were taped to the kitchen walls, and there were child safety locks on cupboards. It looked okay from outside—just like a regular brick house—and it had only six residents, all brain-injured adults. Emma was the youngest and the only one who didn't use a wheelchair. She could walk okay, though her muscles are tight and she kind of walks on her toes. Her left side drags a bit, but she manages.

Mom said this residence was really good and that we were lucky to get Emma placed here. Even after a year, though, Emma was always asking when she could come back home. To be honest, this place didn't feel like a home to me either. It made me antsy.

"Let's go to the coffee shop, hey?" I tilted my head and smiled at Em's skinny face.

"I want French fries."

"Sure."

"And ketchup."

"You bet." We had French fries and ketchup every Tuesday.

Em clutched my arm, and we walked out together. Guilt was eating a hole in my stomach. I couldn't imagine telling her we were all going to go off sailing without her. She had no idea how long a year was. Fifty-two Tuesdays on her calendar with no visits. Fifty-two Sundays that she wouldn't be coming home for dinner.

I couldn't believe we were going to do this to her.

Four

A few days before we left, I poked my head into Tim's room. "Done packing?"

He shook his head, looking even more worried than usual. Huge piles of books were spread out all over his floor.

"What are you doing?"

"Sorting."

Tim's room was wall-to-wall books—alphabetized, categorized and organized in a typically neurotic Tim-like fashion. "Why?" I asked.

He shrugged. "Trying to decide what books to bring."

He had a box of large Ziploc bags sitting beside him and had begun to put books into them. History books. Tim's obsessed with history.

He saw me staring and picked up a bag defensively. "Water damage," he said. "In case the air on the boat is too damp."

"You are one strange kid," I said to him. "This is a holiday, you know. Normal people read Stephen King or John Grisham. Not..." I picked up the nearest book. "*Palestine: Peace Not Apartheid.*"

Tim grabbed it back. "So read Stephen King," he said. "If being normal is so important to you."

It's not important to me, I wanted to tell him. It's important to the rest of the world. I could just picture him wandering through the crowded hallway at school, nose in a book, shoulder blades poking out like bird wings under his thin plaid shirt. He'd get pulverized.

Sometimes I thought Tim was more like a little old man than a twelve-year-old boy. Boys his age were supposed to be obsessed with girls, hide *Playboy* magazines under their beds, tell fart jokes and play team sports. They were supposed to practice saying the entire alphabet in one belch and be generally loud and annoying. Well, I guess Tim had the annoying part down, and I had caught him looking at a Victoria's Secret catalog once, but that was about it. The only remotely normal thing he did was rollerblading, but even that was a joke. He was hopeless at it. He would wobble up and down our driveway, waving his arms like he was trying to fly.

Dad, our resident expert on child development, didn't seem to have noticed that Tim was a freak. Apparently neither Tim nor I were quite screwed up enough to hold his interest. I think Dad must have been around more when we were younger. There are family photographs of me riding on his shoulders and of him reading stories to me and Emma. When I look at them, I feel all weird and sort of depressed—like I lost something important, and can't even remember having it.

I don't know if it was the accident that changed things, but as far back as I can remember, he's spent most of his time at the office. When he was home, he'd be busy reading the *Journal of Child and Adolescent Psychology*, or writing articles on self-esteem, resiliency and healthy attachment. If he spoke to us at all, it was usually just to tell us to keep our voices down.

We left one evening in late August. Everyone came down to the dock to wave us off. Well—not everyone. Emma wasn't there: too upsetting for her, Mom and Dad said. Too upsetting for them, more like.

Everyone else was there though. Jen and a bunch of my other friends, boaters from our marina, some of the social workers and psychologists from the children's mental health clinic where Dad works and a ton of Mom's friends.

Jen pulled me aside. "Shit," she said for the thousandth time. "This sucks. Seriously. You can't go away for a whole year."

"I know. I know."

"We had so many plans for next year. I mean, grade eleven is supposed to be the best. You're gonna miss so much."

"Tell me about it." My chest was all tight and achy.

"God, I'm going to miss you," she whispered. She pushed the neatly coiled dock line with the toe of her sneaker.

"I'll miss you too."

"No you won't. You'll be too busy partying with gorgeous boys on sunny beaches."

I giggled. "Shh. Don't tell my parents." I made a face. "Don't forget about me, okay?"

"Not a chance. You better stay in touch, Rachel. I mean it."

I'd had a huge fight with Dad about bringing a laptop. He'd said he wanted to "get away from all that," like there was some great virtue in being out of touch with the rest of the world. Mom had been on my side—it would have made taking correspondence courses way easier, for one thing—but we'd lost. "I'll e-mail whenever I can," I told Jen. "I promise."

She hesitated; then she grabbed me and gave me an awkward hug. "Look, you can always come back and stay with me. You know. If things don't work out."

Mom was watching us. My parents don't trust Jen, mainly because she lived in a group home for a while last year. Dad's a total hypocrite. If Jen were one of his clients, he'd rattle on about the resilience and courage of what he calls "youth with challenges." But since she's my friend, she's just a bad influence.

"Rachel? Can you join the rest of us?" Dad beckoned. He was standing at the bow of the boat, and I could tell he was about to make ones of his speeches.

Jen and I shuffled back into the crowd. I stared at my sneakers, white against the rough brown wood of the dock.

Dad cleared his throat. "It's wonderful to have so many of you here to see us off," he said. "Our network of friends—our extended family. Thank you all for being a part of this wonderful adventure and wishing us well as we set sail for new horizons. Life is what you make it, and we are choosing to pursue our dreams. I hope that you will all do the same, whatever your dreams may be."

Jen caught my eye, and I poked my finger in my mouth and pretended to gag. Dad was so embarrassing.

People on the dock were starting to fidget and look at their watches.

"I have a surprise for you all," he said. He moved to the bow of the boat and put his hands on a cloth that was draped over the lifelines.

I hadn't noticed it before.

"In honor of this occasion, I'd like to have a naming ceremony." He whisked the cloth away, revealing new black letters on the boat's hull. Apparently the *Wind Weaver* was now called *Shared Dreams*.

I folded my arms and said nothing. I'd liked the old name.

Dad cracked a bottle of champagne over the bow rail and let the spray wash across the deck, completely oblivious to the irony of his single-handedly changing the boat's name. *Shared Dreams*—not likely.

Tim nudged me. "It's bad luck to change a boat's name," he whispered.

We spent the entire fall—when I should have been starting grade eleven and hanging out with Jen—slogging through the canals from Ontario to New York, and then on down the Intra-Coastal Waterway.

Of course, if you sailed in the ocean it would take only a week. On the ICW, it took months. Delaware, Maryland, Virginia, North Carolina, South Carolina, Georgia, Florida. We motored along winding rivers, slowly accumulating mile after mile on the odometer and staying right on Dad's schedule to reach the Bahamas in early December. Every day he charted our slow progress, and a wiggly pencil line crept inch by inch along the chart. Five miles an hour. Pretty much like walking from Canada to the Bahamas, if you thought about it. I tried not to.

Mom flew home from Florida to visit Emma, while Dad, Tim and I stayed and got the boat ready for the big crossing to the islands. We rented a car and bought whole cases of beans, tuna, chick peas, toilet paper and pop. The boat was so full of stuff that it was sitting a good couple of inches lower in the water. We re-sealed leaky stanchions, changed oil and fuel filters, and cleaned and refilled the water tanks. It was a ton of work, but it wasn't as if there was much else to do: We were miles up some creek and stuck in a tiny marina where there was no one even close to my age to talk to.

Most of the trip had been kind of boring, to be honest. Mile after mile of canal with nothing to look at except the odd pelican diving for a fish.

Dad lost it every time Tim or I dared to suggest it wasn't totally thrilling.

"How can you call this boring?" he demanded. "You've traveled through nine states; you've seen dolphins leaping out of the water right beside the boat—"

"Yeah, like twice," I said. "That was cool. But come on. That was maybe fifteen minutes of dolphins out of three months of steering in a straight line and staying between the red and green markers."

"Most kids would give anything for an opportunity like this." He had that look on his face like he was about to start talking about the lousy lives of the kids he works with. Sometimes I envied those kids. Maybe if your whole family was screwed up—I mean, obviously screwed up, on the outside, not just secretly screwed up like our family— then maybe there'd be less pressure to be so freaking perfect. Maybe people wouldn't expect you to be happy and grateful all the time.

I shrugged. "I'm just saying that motoring down a canal for ten hours at a time isn't exactly a thrill, okay?"

He shook his head. "Your frame of mind is directly related to your attitude. You choose to be bored, instead of appreciating what the day has to bring."

Dad was big on inspirational sayings. He was always going on about "living in the moment." He had taped quotes up all over the boat, just like he used to do at home. Above the table where Tim and I do our homework: *Study as if you were to live forever. Live as if you were going to die tomorrow.* By the navigation instruments: *We are here and the time is now*. They were scattered everywhere: reminders, Dad said, for us to be present. *Do not dwell in the past, do not dream of the future, concentrate the mind on the present moment. When you are in the moment you are truly alive. Being in the moment means being aware and living in the flow of life*. Etcetera, etcetera.

You'd think with all those reminders, I'd be able to do it. But the truth is, when I'm not remembering the things that have already happened, I'm worrying about what's going to happen next.

Anyway, the crossing to the Bahamas was hellish. We left the day after Mom came back, and it was really rough. Mom and I threw up the whole way. And it took forever, since Dad didn't want to stop at the Berry Islands and insisted on going all the way to Nassau. A day and night and another day, non-stop puking. How's that for quality family time?

I hate that it's always me and Mom who get sick. It seems so stereotypical—like women are weaker or something, which is such bullshit. I'm small—small for my age, everyone said, until I was about twelve and it became obvious that it wasn't going to be a temporary state—but I'm stronger than Tim and a better sailor too. He's always off in his head, thinking about the Second World War or about the conflict in the Middle East, totally oblivious to the fact that the sails need trimming or the boat is off course. But for some reason, motion doesn't bother him. While I'm popping Gravol and staring grimly at the horizon, he sits down below and reads history books.

By the time we finally got to Nassau and cleared customs, I was weirdly tired and hungry and hyper, all at once. I went off for a walk by myself. And that was when I met Will and Sheila for the first time.

I was walking down the main drag, which seemed to be a long row of liquor stores and souvenir trash, when a voice behind me said, "Ahoy, *Shared Dreams.*"

I spun around. A couple about my parents' age, with dark tans, loud T-shirts and lots of gold jewelry, were walking behind me.

"Hi," I said uncertainly.

"Hey." The man stuck out his hand. "We just met your folks. We're on *Freebird*. You know, the trawler in the slip beside you at the marina."

"Oh. Hi."

They were both grinning like I was their long lost daughter.

"We told your folks we'd keep an eye out for you," the man said. "I'm Will. This is my wife, Sheila."

Sheila smiled. She was blond, with dark sunglasses and those beaded braids that tourists apparently feel compelled to get whenever they go anywhere with a beach.

"Nice to meet you," I said politely. "I'm sure I'll see you around."

Will winked at me. Good looking, but one of those guys who are always trying to seem younger and cooler than they really are. He reminded me of this guidance counselor at my school who was always bringing in his guitar and joking around like he was one of the students. Nice enough, but a bit of a goof.

Anyway, that's all history. It's been a month since I met Will and Sheila in Nassau. A whole lifetime ago. Believe it or not, things are actually a whole lot more messed up now. At least with history, no matter how awful it is, you already know what happened.

So now here we are. Limping back to Georgetown with a cracked rudder and no idea what is going to happen next.

Five

I eye the low profile of Great Exuma Island, and my stomach tightens. The green hills are speckled with little pastel squares: the houses of Georgetown.

It is late afternoon, and the clouds cast shadows on the water; their dark shapes are indistinguishable from the coral heads that lie beneath the surface, waiting to tear apart the thin fibreglass hull that holds our home together.

"It's too late," I tell Dad. "It'll be too hard to navigate." My hand is sweaty on the wheel.

Dad looks up at the sky, shades his eyes with his hand. "The sun's not that low in the sky."

I give the wheel an experimental wiggle. "I don't trust the steering. It feels all wrong."

"There's a big crack in the rudder," he says. "Of course it feels wrong. It got us this far, it held together all night long. It'll last another half hour."

I exchange glances with Tim.

"Let's look on the bright side," Dad says cheerfully. "We're lucky the damage isn't worse."

If only we hadn't hit the rocks, we'd be sailing in the opposite direction. If only Long Island's marina hadn't been wiped out in the last hurricane, we could have got the rudder fixed there. If only, if only, if only.

I look at Georgetown, slowly but inevitably getting closer. I didn't expect to be coming back. Didn't ever want to see this place again.

Mom doesn't say anything, just gazes at the harbor entrance. I wonder what she is thinking. I couldn't tell how she felt about leaving Georgetown, and I can't tell now how she feels about going back. Excited? Anxious? I have no idea.

I don't even know who she is anymore.

I stand up and look at Dad. "Fine. You can take us in then. I'm not doing it."

He shakes his head. "Look, I know you're nervous. We're all shaky from hitting those rocks. But it's your watch, and I know you can do this."

I shake my head stubbornly. "I'm not doing it." It's not the navigation or the visibility that is worrying me. It's this: When everything falls apart, I don't want to have been the one who guided our boat back to the place where the unraveling began.

"Rachel. I don't want to make a big deal of this, but it is about responsibility," Dad says. "We all agreed on a rotating watch system while we're at sea. It's your watch from one PM until three PM."

"I'm not doing it," I say again.

He puts on his disappointed-parent expression.

"We're a team out here, Rachel. You know that. And a chain is only as strong as its weakest link."

Tim stands up. "I'll do it, Rach."

My jaw practically drops. Tim and I have never talked about what happened last time we were here. Does Nerd Boy actually understand why I don't want to do this? Or is he just looking to score some points with Dad?

"Cheers," I say, letting him take the wheel from me. I don't even look at Dad as I walk past him and up to the foredeck.

The wind blows my hair off my face as I stare at the water ahead. To be honest, the unraveling of our family probably began long before what happened in Georgetown. I can try to sift backward through the layers of the past, but I can't identify the point at which things started to go wrong. Emma moving out, Dad spending all his time at the office, all the fights between him and Mom. Were things okay before all of that? When we were younger? I thought so, but maybe little kids always do. Maybe as long as no one is hitting or shouting, as long as there's food to eat and toys to play with, kids always think their family is just dandy.

I was four and Emma was six when she had her accident. She was in hospital for months, but I don't remember any of that. I didn't really understand that there was anything wrong with her until my friends started asking questions. To me, she was just Em. I knew she couldn't talk as well as me, and I knew she was different, but none of that means much when you're a little kid.

As I got older, Mom started to tell me more. I knew that Emma's brain had been damaged, and that the doctors hadn't even known if she'd ever come out of the coma. I knew that when she started walking and talking again, everyone said it was a miracle. And I knew that as she got older, it had slowly become clear that the miracle hadn't been quite enough. Emma had seizures, even with the medication she took every day. Dad started talking about developmental milestones and how Emma wasn't meeting them. She was having all kinds of difficulties with learning and memory and behavior. She was in a special class at school.

Em was the oldest, but Tim and I caught up with her and overtook her and treated her like she was the baby of the family. I've always felt kind of guilty about that. About being able to do so many things that she couldn't do.

Sometimes I wonder if guilt about the accident was what started the unraveling for Mom and Dad. It wasn't something either of them ever talked about.

Tim guides the boat back in the southeastern entrance of Elizabeth Harbor, carefully navigating between reefs and shoals and taking us back to Georgetown.

The harbor is huge: nine miles long, a narrow channel running between the barrier islands and the south end of Great Exuma Island, which is practically the southernmost island in a chain of hundreds. Most of them are inhabited

only by iguanas, so Georgetown is pretty much a metrop-
olis by local standards. It has a few hundred residents,
a hotel, several restaurants and bars and a tiny library.
In the winter, the boats flood in. Hundreds of boats. The
population of Georgetown doubles.

Once we're in the harbor, I go back to the cockpit. Tim
and I argue that we should anchor in Kidd Cove, to be
close to town, or over near Volleyball Beach. Anywhere
but Red Shanks. Of course, we can't say why, and Dad
overrules us.

"Maybe our spot will still be there," he says.

He's all excited, and I feel weird about it. Sort of embarrassed for him and angry that he can be so oblivious. He's
the only one who doesn't know. The only one for whom
Red Shanks is just a beautiful secluded anchorage and
nothing more.

Dad takes the helm, and Tim and I drop the sails. Mom
is up on the bow, reading the depth of the water by the
shade of blue, using hand signals to direct Dad. People go
aground in here all the time, but it's a soft sandy bottom.
If you get stuck, you just wait for the tide to lift you free.

In the end, I'm the one who lowers the heavy plough
anchor. Right where we were before, in the innermost part of
the anchorage. The same three sailboats sit quietly in the still
shallow water. The trawler *Freebird*, Will and Sheila's boat, is
tucked into the back corner where the water is too shallow
for most sailboat keels. It hasn't budged since we left.

The water is a crystal-clear turquoise. The slight hint of
green in the blueness means it's less than eight feet deep.

I can see the anchor settling into the sand even before Dad puts the engine in reverse. The boat tugs against the anchor chain, and I watch the shoreline. We're not moving. I give a thumbs-up signal to let Dad know the anchor is set.

Back in the cockpit, Dad gives Tim a high five and then a big pat on the back. "Great job, Tim. Thanks for taking the helm and bringing the boat in. Nice work."

He's talking to Tim, but he keeps looking at me. It's all about making me feel bad, not about Tim doing a good job at all.

"It is a relief to be anchored safely," Mom says. "I was a little nervous, I have to admit. If the rudder had fallen off out there in the Sound…" She is looking back the way we came, toward the rough, dark blue water of Exuma Sound.

"I knew it'd be fine," Dad says. "We were all upset by the little incident at Long Island, but we pulled together and we made it back here just fine." He nods and looks at me again. "This is a good example of how we choose our experiences. You can give in to the failure messages and make excuses. Not be willing to try. Or you can choose to be positive and greet life's experiences eagerly."

I roll my eyes and lean back against the bulkhead. "Can we go ashore? I think my leg muscles are atrophying from being stuck on the boat."

"We should wait and make sure the anchor is set properly," Dad says.

Mom stands up and stretches. "How about you and Tim stay on the boat? Rachel and I will dinghy over to town and see if we can arrange to get the boat hauled out tomorrow. Get that rudder fixed as soon as possible." She shrugs. "We can pick up some provisions too. Maybe we'll only need to be here for a couple of days."

I exchange glances with Tim. It sounds like Mom is as eager to get out of here as we are.

I guess that's a good thing.

Six

Mom and I scramble into the dinghy and head toward town. Neither of us says much, which is kind of how things are with us these days.

I used to feel like we knew each other better than anyone else. When I was little, she'd just look at my face when I came home from school and know what kind of day I'd had. She was the kind of mom who would dress up as a cowboy with us, didn't mind if we wanted to eat nothing but cream cheese on toast for a week, was happy to cut our sandwiches into triangles instead of squares and gave us Pooh-bear stickers for remembering to floss. All my friends thought she was the greatest.

I don't know exactly when things started to change. Just the last couple of years, I guess. Tim and I outgrew cowboys and triangular food—though Emma still likes that stuff—and Mom found other things to do. Volunteering for the community living association, raising money for programs for special needs kids, organizing community awareness campaigns. More and more, she'd ask Tim and me to look after Emma while she went out to meetings. She started running too. Rain, snow, whatever—she'd be out there practically every evening, racing like a long-legged greyhound on the sidewalks around town.

Then Emma moved out, and everything started to change. I began grade ten and met Jen and started wanting my own life. All of a sudden, everything was a fight. My hair, my clothes, my friends, my music, my curfew. It was like Mom and Dad didn't want me to grow up.

Still, even when we were fighting all the time, I never wondered who Mom really was. I thought I knew her.

I look at her sitting across from me in the dinghy, her sun-streaked hair blowing loose from under her base-ball cap, her teeth white in her tanned face. She's grinning widely. One hand is on the tiller of the outboard engine, and with the other hand she's trying to catch her hair and tuck it under her hat. We're going full speed, with the bow of our little Zodiac lifted up as we skim across the smooth water.

Toward Georgetown.

Mom slows the engine as we approach the dinghy dock in Kidd Cove. I lean over the side and grab the dock as the dinghy bumps to a stop. She cuts the engine. The silence between us is thick, solid, impenetrable.

I wonder if things will ever feel normal again.

I tie the dinghy up, and we step out of the boat. The wooden dock scorches the soles of my feet. "Crap," I mutter.

"What?"

I point down. "I left my shoes on the boat."

Mom starts to laugh. "Oh my god, I did too."

We look at each other; then we look at the sun-baked road stretching up and over the hill.

I start to giggle. "We can't walk to the grocery store without shoes."

"No."

I don't want to go back to the boat, but the ground is too hot to stand still. I hop back and forth, one foot to the other. "What do you want to do?"

She nods toward the Two Turtles Inn. "I'll buy you a drink. And then we'll go sort out the details for getting the boat fixed."

"A drink? Really? An actual, cold, drink?" I open my eyes wide, goofing a little. "With ice cubes?"

Mom grins at me. "With ice cubes."

I hesitate. "Is there a catch?"

"Yeah." She nods. "You tell me what's going on."

My heart slams against my rib cage and my mouth is instantly sand dry. "What do you mean?"

Her eyes are narrow, green, long lashed. The same eyes Tim and Emma have. I got stuck with Dad's: dark brown and too round. Dog eyes.

"You know what I mean. You and Tim have been acting strange for days."

I shrug. "I don't know. Nothing's going on." I look away from her, out into the harbor. Pale yellow in the shallows, shading into green, turquoise, clear blue, deep sky blue.

She is quiet for a moment; then she sighs and shrugs, her shoulders slumped. There are dark shadows under her eyes. "I wish you'd talk to me."

No she doesn't. She really doesn't. My sunglasses slip on my sweaty face, and I push them on more firmly. I wish she'd stop asking me. "There's nothing to say," I tell her. "Nothing to talk about."

The next day, we slip back into the Georgetown routine as if we'd never left. Dad flips on the VHF and tunes into the cruisers' net on channel 68 before Tim or I are even out of bed. I pull a pillow over my head and groan as the sound of Will's voice, slightly static but relentlessly jovial, fills the cabin. Every morning, I realize, for as long as we are here, my day will begin with Will's voice saying, "Good morning, Georgetown!"

Will is the host of the Georgetown cruisers' net. It's like our own little radio show—the Georgetown morning show—and you know that every single person on the four hundred or so boats here will be listening. First, the weather, which in sailing terms means the wind: how much and from which direction. Then the local businesses get on the radio and advertise. The owner of Eddie's Edgewater actually sings a little jingle. Next the cruisers all call in from their boats, making announcements: some couple has just arrived and wants to send out "a big howdy" to everyone here, a guy is flying back to the States and will take your mail if you drop it off at his boat today, someone needs a zinc for his propeller shaft, a volleyball game is happening this afternoon on Volleyball Beach, someone on a boat called the *Message of Love* is hosting a Christian Fellowship meeting tonight.

Finally, half an hour later, the broadcast ends with a Thought for the Day. Today's thought, Will says, is this: *Our futures hinge on each of a thousand choices. Living is making choices.* Where does he find this stuff?

Right up Dad's alley, that one. He practically scrambles across the table, trying to find a pen so he can write it down and stick it on the wall.

Choices. Right. I feel like throwing up.

Dad spends the day arguing with the workers at the boatyard. It seems we won't be hauled out until tomorrow. So we spend the day doing the usual things: schoolwork and boat maintenance. A nine-to-five workday.

"I don't feel like studying," I grumble to Tim. "Don't you want to get off the boat?"

He shrugs and looks up from his book. "I guess. But it's like Dad says: If we only worked when we felt like it, we'd never get much done."

"Shut up."

We sit in silence for a while. I shake my nail polish bottle and unscrew the lid. Black to match my hair.

I start to paint my nails. I can tell Tim's not actually reading because he isn't turning pages.

"Mom's acting weird," he says at last.

"Duh. Anyway, I told you I don't want to talk about what happened."

"Yeah, but…she keeps staring at me and looking like she might cry."

I think about that for a minute. Mom had been acting kind of strange even before Georgetown. Ever since Emma moved out, I guess. She'd been kind of spaced out—there but not really there. I'd figured she wasn't as excited about the trip as Dad was and was just going along with it because that's what she does. Tim was right though. Lately she'd been kind of…emotional, I guess. Like, last night she told me she loved me, for no reason at all. I guess that sounds nice, but we're not the kind of family that says stuff like that a lot. Besides, I figured it was motivated by guilt, and I wasn't in the mood to hear it.

"I don't know," I say. "She's fucked up. Obviously."

"Do you think they're going to get divorced?"

"Damn." I grab a Kleenex and dab at my cuticle. "Look what you made me do."

"Do you think they are going to get divorced?" Tim repeats.

"I heard you." I look up from my nails and scowl at him. Like I need more to worry about. "How should I know?"

Tim doesn't say anything.

I shrug, feeling bad again. As usual.

The daily routine continues. Every day at four thirty at the Red Shanks anchorage, everyone meets on the beach for drinks. The beach is a tiny patch of sand and on nights like tonight, when the tide is high, there is no beach at all. The water goes right up to the dense scrubby trees. You'd think this might pose a challenge to the happy hour hoopla, but no. Nothing comes between these people and their drinks. So everyone stands around, ankle deep in water, downing their gin and tonics or rum and Cokes like it's totally freaking normal. They call it the Red Shanks Yacht and Tennis Club.

I guess it's supposed to be a joke.

Some joke. All these middle-aged couples dressed up and standing around in the ocean getting pissed. It's totally depressing.

Anyway, I'm not really in the mood, but Mom and Dad and Tim are all going, and I don't want to be stuck on the boat. There's only one dinghy, so if I don't go ashore with them, I'm not going anywhere. Besides, I don't want to miss anything.

I quickly brush my teeth and put on a little lip gloss. Makeup seems a bit pointless when you are living on a boat and have to wash your hair in salt water half the time. (Plus, the bathroom on the boat—officially known as The Head—is about two feet by two feet, has a tiny mirror that gives my face a strange green tint and is generally not a place you want to spend any more time than necessary.) Still, you never know when someone interesting might show up.

Of course, I haven't actually seen a guy my age for over a month, and if one showed up now, I'd probably be too nervous to talk to him. I wrinkle my nose at my reflection. Freckles. Hundreds of them. Thousands. All over my entire face and most of my body too. Unfortunately, that's what Tim and I do instead of tanning.

Mom scavenges around in one of the lockers and finds a bag of BBQ chips that we brought from the States; Dad grabs a couple of room-temperature Kaliks; and we all climb into the dinghy. One happy family going to a beach party on a non-existent beach.

It's only a short ride. As we get closer, I see Will and Sheila. Sheila is fully clothed for once and showing off her tan in a sleeveless white top and a short denim skirt. A bunch of other couples, most of them in cargo shorts and T-shirts, mill around in the water, all with drinks in hand.

The dinghy bottom scrapes the sand and we all get out, barefoot in the warm water. I grab the dinghy line and tie it to a tree branch on the shore. Then I turn around and look at my family. Mom is hanging back a little, her expression guarded. Dad is looking around for someone to talk to. His speeches are bad enough when he's sober, but once he's had a couple drinks, I avoid him. I suspect I am not the only one. Tim looks like he always does: glasses glinting in the setting sun, his baseball cap on totally straight and his shirt tucked into his shorts. He's standing between Mom and Dad like he's the glue holding them together.

Maybe he is.

"Hey there, you crazy Canadians," says a voice.

I turn around. It's Mango, his hair straggling over his shoulders, the top of his balding head sunburned and peeling. Mango lives here, I guess. He says he came here from Delaware ten years ago and never left. I don't know what he does for money. Not that he seems to have much.

Tim grins and relaxes. "Hey."

Within two minutes, Mango has mooched a beer off Dad and is deep in discussion with Tim. They seem to be talking about resistance movements and the rescue of Danish Jews during the second World War.

Dad wanders off to find someone to bore. I stand beside Mom, feeling a bit lost. Above us on the low cliff edge sits Grace, a driftwood and coconut mannequin who, like most of the cruisers here, looks like she's spent a little too much time in the sun. Her stick arms are bleached white and one of her coconuts has slipped down so she's slightly lop-sided. A sign on the shore beside her reads: *Red Shanks Yacht and Tennis Club Rules: Rule One—when Grace starts looking good, it's time to leave.* Which says all you need to know about this place. It's like a summer camp for seniors.

Will and Sheila wave and then splash over to join us.

"What are you doing back here?" Will asks. "I thought you were heading to the Turks and Caicos."

Mom gives him a rueful grin. "So did we." She laughs, like it's no big deal that we came back. "We had a close encounter with some rocks at Long Island."

Will groans. "Ohhh…Not good."

"You're all okay, though?' Sheila asks.

Mom nods. "It wasn't dangerous. I mean, we were practically on shore—well, that was the problem really. We misjudged a turn and got in too close."

"We cracked the rudder," I say, watching Mom's face. "We have to haul out to get it fixed. So I guess we'll be stuck back here for a few days at least."

Will and Sheila are smiling and nodding.

"Well, that's nice for us," Will says. "This place wouldn't be half as much fun without you."

I can't believe his nerve. I grit my teeth and look around for an excuse to wander off. To my relief I see someone I know: Becca, wading through the water carrying a huge bowl of popcorn.

I wave and start splashing in her direction. "Becca! Hey!"

"Hey, Rachel." She tilts her head. "I thought you guys were leaving."

"Yeah, well. We came back." I don't feel like explaining all over again, but I give her a condensed version of what happened. I feel a bit shy around Becca. She's the only person here who's even close to my age, but most of the time when I see her, I'm with my family. I don't want her to think I'm just a kid.

Mom keeps glancing over. My parents don't trust Becca any more than they trusted Jen. Becca is nineteen (too old for me), has bleached blond dreadlocks and a pierced nose (evidence of delinquency), and is here by herself, on her own twenty-six-foot Contessa (no parental supervision). Also she goes to the bars to see the Rake-and-Scrape bands every Monday and Thursday and is friends with the local guys. Mom and Dad won't let me go to the Rake-and-Scrapes with her because, they say, there'll be drinking there. Which is true, but that doesn't mean I'd have to drink.

Anyway, given that I am surrounded right now by adults getting drunk, this last argument seems somewhat hypocritical. I think that the issue is more about the local guys. Some cruisers, like Mango, get really involved in the local community. He brings supplies for the school, helps out at the food bank and hangs around with some of the residents. Others—like my parents—do not. They pretend they're too busy with boat maintenance and cruiser events, but the truth is they're just uncomfortable with the locals. Well, Dad is anyway. I didn't realize it before this trip, but he's kind of racist. I guess when he decided to take us all to the Bahamas, he'd forgotten that most of the people here are black.

"So…you're getting hauled out tomorrow?" Becca gestures in the direction of the boatyard. "You going to be here long?"

I shrug. "Dunno."

She takes her sunglasses off and hangs them on her T-shirt, one black plastic arm slipped inside the V-neck. Her nose is small and a little flat, her face wide and tanned an even brown. She flashes me a grin. "There's a band playing at Eddie's tomorrow night. A Rake-and-Scrape band. You should come."

"No chance. My parents won't let me." I make a face to show that I know how pathetic this is.

"Well…I'll be there, if they change their minds."

It's the first time in months that I've been invited to do something without my family. I look around and see Dad chatting with an older man. They are both wearing the exact same khaki cargo shorts. Mom's still standing where I left her, talking to Will and Sheila. I'm desperate to get away from all of them, and I wonder if there's a way I could go out without Mom and Dad knowing. "Okay," I tell Becca. "I'll come if I can."

We all go back to the boat for dinner, and then Mom and Dad go over to *Freebird* to watch a movie. Tim goes with them, still trying to be the glue, still trying to hold the family together. When he's anxious about something, he can't leave it alone. When I'm anxious about something, I avoid it.

Just like Mom.

Anyway, it's a relief to be alone on the boat. I'm looking forward to tomorrow, when *Shared Dreams* gets hauled out. We'll be living "on the hard"—on hard ground instead of water. Climbing up or down a ladder between the boat and the boatyard whenever we want to go anywhere. At least for a few days I'll be able to come and go without having to negotiate the use of the dinghy.

That'll be more freedom than I've had in months.

I lie down on my parents' bed—it's the V-berth, in the bow of the boat. My own bed gets dismantled every morning to make room for the table, and Tim's is just a tiny berth in the aft cabin, crammed full of stuff whenever he's not actually using it. I close my eyes, and I guess I doze off because when I open them again, Tim and my parents are climbing down the companionway steps. It's dark, and I can hear rain falling lightly on the deck. I poke my head up through the V-berth hatch.

A few lights twinkle in the town, and lights are scattered here and there throughout Red Shanks. Becca's little boat glows softly, its kerosene anchor light swinging from the boom. Over on *Freebird,* a deck light shines brightly. No doubt my parents had a fine time watching some bad action flick with Will and Sheila and playing at being happy couples.

I think about that moment with Mom today, when she asked what was wrong. I wonder what she would have said if I'd told her the truth.

Seven

The next morning our boat is hauled out of the water. This presents some definite possibilities. All day I think about Becca's invitation.

The thing is, I don't actually break my parents' rules very often. Kids back home would be surprised to hear this. You dye your hair black and get a bit mouthy with teachers, and everyone assumes you just do whatever the hell you please, that you don't let anyone tell you what to do. If you don't go to a party, they think it's because you have something better—more hard-core—to do.

They don't assume you're at home babysitting your older sister. They don't guess that parties packed with kids laughing and making out make you so uncomfortable you end up drinking yourself sick.

Even Jen. I mean, she's my best friend, but she doesn't really know me as well as she thinks she does. We only met last year, at the start of grade ten. I was still hanging out with my old friends from elementary school, going to the mall and having sleepover parties, feeling a bit bored and restless but not knowing why. Then Jen showed up, a group home kid with multiple piercings and an attitude to match. She kind of picked me out of the crowd, and we fell into being best friends.

I've never told Jen the truth about Emma's accident, or about Mom and Dad's fights. Still, I miss her. I miss all the laughing and teasing and gossiping. I miss the fun.

To hell with your parents, she'd say. Go to the damn party. Go find Becca and party your ass off.

Maybe I will.

Shared Dreams is balanced high above the asphalt on a cradle of wood and steel, a long ladder balanced against her stern for us to climb up and down. It feels strange to be sitting up here, crowded around the dinner table. I can see why they call it being on the hard: that's exactly how it feels, stiff and unyielding, after four months afloat. On the wall above the table hangs a framed copy of our family mission statement. Dad made us write it before we left on this trip. It starts with *Building our Lives through Conscious Choices* and ends with *Loving Concern and Honesty Toward Each Other*. Hah.

As usual, dinner is a combination of potatoes, onions, tiny local green peppers and canned chicken that we brought from home, by the caseload. Sometimes there's fresh fish instead, usually grouper, and sometimes a can of chickpeas—we still have about a year's supply of those.

And that's about it. You can't get much here, and it's all crazy expensive. A single red pepper, if you can find one, costs about six bucks. A gallon of milk is nine.

Dad's had too much beer over at the Two Turtles Inn, and he's in a rotten mood. He starts out by grumbling about the food. "Christ, Laura, can't you use some spices or something? Do something different with the potatoes?"

Mom shrugs. "You want to take over the cooking, be my guest. If you're sick of eating it, I'm just as sick of cooking it."

I wish Dad would shut up. In theory, he's all about gender equality—he's even given talks about it at conferences: *Challenging Gendered Expectations in the School System.* That was the last one. But cook a meal himself? Not likely.

He stabs at his potatoes with his fork. "And you'll deal with the guys in the boatyard, will you? Because I'm not just sitting around doing nothing, you know." He shakes his head. "I'm telling you, if you don't stay on those guys, they'll never get around to doing anything."

None of us say anything. As far as I can see, our rudder still hasn't been touched. I suspect this is because of Dad's nagging, not in spite of it.

"Have they given you a timeline?" Mom asks. "Do they know when they'll be able to get to it?"

"Timeline? Timeline? They don't know the meaning of the word. They just want our money, that's all. They just want to charge us for sitting here in this goddamn parking lot, night after night."

"Oh, Mitch, I'm sure that's not true."

He pushes his plate away. "You don't know these people like I do, Laura. You can't trust them."

I hate it when he starts talking like this. I feel embarrassed for him. Maybe I should try turning one of his own lines back on him. *Just focus your energy on staying positive and hopeful, Dad. Remember, how you feel is directly related to the thoughts you choose to have.* Hah. That'd go over well.

"I was thinking about going out tonight," I say instead. "With Becca."

As a conversation stopper, I couldn't have picked anything more effective. Mom and Dad both turn to me.

"Honey, I don't know about that," Mom says. "We don't really know her that well, and she's a lot older than you. Where were you thinking of going?"

"Eddie's Edgewater," I say. "There's a live band. Local music."

Dad snorts. "Local guys, more like. Sorry, Rachel, the answer is no. I'm not comfortable with you hanging around there, especially when there's drinking."

I snap. "You don't seem to have a problem with me being around people who are drinking, as long as they're old and white."

There is a terrible silence. I have said something unforgivable. I have forgotten the rule: If you can't say anything nice, don't say anything at all.

Tim stares at me, eyes wide.

Mom's cheeks are pink, and she pushes a plate across the table. "More potatoes, anyone?" she says.

Dad just stands up and walks away. Out into the cockpit, down the ladder. Gone.

And I realize that I'm still on Mom's side. I shouldn't be. But I am.

A rush of anger floods through me, and I have to look away. I can't stand to be around her right now. To hell with Family Time and Family Mission Statements and all the rest of it. Maybe I should just do whatever I want. Maybe I should just tell lies like everyone else.

So before I get into bed, I put on some makeup and find my flashlight. Then I lie under the covers and wait for my parents to go to sleep.

Eight

Eddie's is dark and noisy and crowded. It smells like booze and cigarettes and sweaty bodies crowded together, and the beat of the music thumps inside my chest.

I can't see Becca anywhere.

I need something to do, so I make my way through the crowd, over to the bar, and order two Kaliks. Dad was right to be worried about me coming here. It feels like something inside me is going to explode. I lean against the wall, chug the first beer quickly and start on the second.

The band consists of four guys with a weird assortment of instruments. A big man with a green hat is scraping a metal file along the edge of a saw, and another is playing what looks like a washtub. But one guy, a chubby kid with the worst buck teeth I've ever seen, is wailing away on an electric guitar, and another has what I think is a saxophone.

I listen to a few songs, feeling restless and awkward being there on my own. Still no sign of Becca. Ten more minutes, I tell myself, and then I'll go back home. Back to *Shared Dreams*.

Then I see Will and Sheila, out there on the dance floor. Sheila's blond hair is unbraided and it falls halfway down her back. Even though it's a fast song, her arms are wrapped around Will's neck.

And that day comes flooding back. I don't think I'll ever be able to forget a single detail of it.

It was only a week ago. Tim was in the cabin, kneeling on the V-berth and poking his binoculars up through the open hatch. I can even remember what he was wearing: his Albert Einstein T-shirt and blue swim shorts.

"Cut that out," I said. "You want to grow up to be some kind of pervert?"

I jumped lightly down the companionway steps and poured myself a glass of water. It was lukewarm and tasted gross. Free water from the town pump, because Dad refuses to pay sixty cents a gallon for the reverse osmosis water the other cruisers buy. I made a face and stirred in a spoonful of iced tea powder.

"Where's Sheila?" he complained. "It's noon. Peak time for nude sunbathing."

"You're sick," I told him, although I was actually kind of relieved when Tim did any semi-normal adolescent boy stuff. Maybe he wouldn't always be a complete freak after all.

"Sure you don't want a look?" he asked, just to be annoying. He waggled the binoculars at me. "Sure you don't want to take a peek at Will's willy?"

"Gross." I didn't leave though.

Tim lifted the binoculars back up to his eyes. "He's not there anyway. Neither of them are."

I poked my head up through the hatch beside him. Across the anchorage, *Freebird* sat squat and awkward among the slim and sleek sailboats. *Freebird* doesn't move like the rest of the boats: while we all swing with the tides, she has three anchors down and barely budges all winter. Will says that swinging on a single anchor messes up the TV reception he gets from his satellite dish.

"The dinghy's there," I said. "So someone's home."

Tim shrugged, losing interest. "Well, they're not outside."

"Too bad. You'll have to go a few hours without seeing our neighbors naked." I flopped down on the bed and closed my eyes. I felt like having a nap, but it was too freaking hot. Sweat trickled down my neck and stuck my T-shirt to my back.

"Ugh. I'm going for a swim," I said, not moving. "Are you coming?"

He didn't answer.

"What?" I opened my eyes and looked up at him.

His face had gone completely white except for a bright pink patch high on each cheek. "It's Mom," he whispered.

"On *Freebird*?" I ask, surprised. I thought she'd gone for a run.

He nodded, blinking hard.

"So?"

Wordlessly, he handed me the binoculars.

I pulled myself up to my knees, balanced the binoculars on the fibreglass lip of the hatch to steady them. Then I looked over at *Freebird*.

In the cockpit, Will was standing—naked as usual—with a beer in his hand. Behind him, tall and tanned in her bikini top and orange sarong, was our mother. But here is the part that didn't make sense, that still doesn't make sense: Her arms were wrapped around him. As I stared at them, he turned toward her, still in her arms. And then they were, without a doubt, kissing. And his hand was on her ass.

I dropped the binoculars on the bed as if they had burned my hands. I stared at them for a second. I tried to think, but my thoughts were slippery—hot and liquid and dangerous. I picked up the binoculars, slipped them back in their black case and snapped it closed. "We didn't see that, you hear me? We didn't see anything."

Tim stared at me, his green eyes wide and shocked and shiny wet. "But I saw Mom. I saw…"

"Stop it," I said. "Just shut up. We didn't see anything, you understand me?"

I pushed myself away from him, through the cabin and back up the companionway ladder on legs that I couldn't feel. Outside, the breeze cooled my hot cheeks. Without bothering to change out of my shorts and T-shirt, I stepped over the stern rail.

The water was still and clear beneath the boat. I balanced on the bottom rung of the swim ladder and stared into the blue. On the bottom, a small manta ray slowly flapped across the sand.

I leaned forward, suspended in time. As long as I didn't move, I told myself, nothing would change. As long as I could keep this one thing secret. A school of tiny fish appeared from under the boat, and I let myself fall forward, scattering them in a thousand different directions. The water was cold and clean, and I dove deep, swimming down until the pressure in my ears started to hurt.

I kicked hard, shot upward and broke the surface, gasping for breath. Across the anchorage, I could see *Freebird* sitting squat and smug, its satellite dishes flashing in the sun.

A hand touches my shoulder and I jump.

"Are you okay?" Becca shouts over the music. "You don't look so good."

I shake my head and put my half-empty bottle down on a ledge. "I need some fresh air."

Outside, it is cool and dark. I can see the anchor lights of the sailboats twinkling in the harbor. It's quieter, but the music is spilling out the open door, thrumming in my ears.

"You didn't like the band?" Becca asks.

I shrug. "They were all right." It's funny. In there it all seemed too loud and too close, but now I can feel the rhythm of the music, and I can see why everyone was dancing.

Sheila doesn't know, I think, picturing her wrapped tightly around her husband on the dance floor. I wonder if

Will and my mother have already picked up where they left off. I blink back hot tears and take another swig of my beer.

"It's called goombay music," Becca tells me. "It's been around since slavery times. That's why there're homemade instruments. The slaves used whatever they had." She shrugs. "Course, now the bands have electric guitars and everything."

"It was all right," I say again. "I just didn't feel like being there."

"Come with me then," Becca says. "I was going to visit Col. You know Col? Colton?"

I shake my head.

"On *Flyer*? Thirty-foot ketch? Black hull?"

I shake my head again. "Nope."

"He's from Palm Beach. Not much older than me—twenty-five, I think he said." She lowers her voice. "He's loaded—family money, you know? But he's a fun guy. Been here for a couple of weeks, I guess, anchored over in Kidd Cove. Anyway, he's having some people round tonight. A little party." She laughs. "Everyone here who's under forty. All six of us."

I'm about to say no when I imagine sneaking back onto *Shared Dreams* alone. Lying in bed and listening to Mom's soft snores from the V-berth and thinking about what Tim and I saw.

What the hell. "Sure," I say. I take another swig of my beer, which is starting to go down awfully easily; then I follow Becca down the road to the dock where her dinghy is bobbing on the gentle waves. Anxiety is crackling through me. I just want to be distracted from my thoughts.

Nine

Becca dips the oars into the water, pulling hard, rowing us away from the sprinkling of lights on shore and out into the inky darkness of the harbor. The oars stir up trails of phosphorescence. Every stroke leaves a crescent of glowing light, like a million tiny underwater stars. I reach over and dip my hand down beside the dinghy, letting it drag through the cool water and watching liquid sparks drip from my fingertips.

"Magic, isn't it," Becca says softly.

I nod. A hard painful lump swells in my throat. "Yeah."

"You okay?"

I shake my head. "Sort of. Family stuff, you know?"

Becca nods. "Oh yeah. Can't imagine being stuck on a boat with mine." She grins to soften the words. "They're okay. But a boat's a pretty small space."

I nod. Part of me is desperate to tell someone what Tim and I saw, but I feel oddly ashamed of it. I feel like I'm the one who's done something wrong. "It's no big deal," I say.

Col's boat is anchored in Kidd Cove. The water is rougher than in Red Shanks. The wind is blowing from across the wide harbor, and it's a long enough fetch to build up a slight chop. The boats are all rolling gently from side to side. Music drifts from Col's boat. Jack Johnson singing "Sleep through the Static." I can hear it before I see the boat itself. I *love* that song. Jen and I listened to it all the time.

Becca rows us toward the soft glow of a kerosene anchor light swinging below the boom. I pull out my flashlight and dance its light across the boat's dark hull and up over the deck. Two tiny green circles reflect back at me. I hold the light steady, curious. They're cat's eyes: A small black kitten is keeping watch from the cabin roof.

I reach out and grab the boat; then I hold us steady while Becca ties the dinghy to a stern cleat. We both hop aboard, just as a head pokes up through the companionway hatch.

"Hey," a male voice says.

The light streams out of the cabin behind him, so all I can see is his silhouette.

"Hey, Col. This is my friend, Rachel. I didn't think you'd mind."

I can feel his eyes on me, though I still can't see his face. There is a pause and then he says, "No, that's great, Bec," and beckons us to come in.

Down below, his boat is amazing. It is small, but cozy and well-organized. A little hammock filled with bananas, green peppers, onions and tomatoes hangs above the port berth, and a neat row of books lines a shelf on the starboard side. Brightly colored fabrics—orange, green, blue—cover the upholstery, and soft lights make it all glow. Somehow, his boat feels like a home, whereas ours—which is much bigger—is cramped and dirty and overflowing with stuff. Though of course, there are four of us on *Shared Dreams*. Four people's books, clothes, dirty laundry. Four people's baggage.

Col notices me looking around. "What do you think?"

"I love it." A perfectly round porthole is open above the galley sink, and a breeze blows through. I lift my face to it and breathe deeply. For the first time, I wonder what it would be like to be in the Bahamas on my own, like Becca is. And Col.

"Here," Col says. "Have a drink." He hands me and Bec each a drink—something orange, in tall plastic cups. I sit carefully on the port berth, holding my drink in two hands and feeling like a little kid.

"Just Tang and rum," he says apologetically. "Sorry, no ice."

"Not for me," Becca says. She's still standing, and she shifts her feet impatiently. "Where is everyone?"

He shrugs and puts her drink down on the counter. "I tried to radio you, but I guess you'd already gone into town. Jon and Katie moved their boat down to Sand Dollar Beach just before sunset, so they won't be coming. And I thought Terry was coming but…"

She shakes her head. "He's hanging out with some friends tonight; they're at Eddie's."

"It's just us then," Col says, stating the obvious.

Col notices me staring at his boat and tells me he gutted it and rebuilt the whole interior himself. It's full of clever little hidden storage spaces—behind the cushions, under the floor boards, beneath every surface. Unexpected doors open everywhere.

"How come you named her *Flyer*?" I ask. The words are barely out of my mouth when I remember what Becca told me: He's a pilot.

He grins. "Because I love flying."

"Like passenger planes?"

"Not yet. I'm working on getting my license." He swirls his drink around in the cup. "So far I've only flown small planes."

I can tell that Becca is bored. She's only half listening. I think she was hoping for a party, and now she's trying to figure out how soon we can leave without being rude. Col doesn't seem to notice.

"Let's sit outside," he says. "It's a gorgeous night."

Becca sits beside him. I take a seat across the cockpit and stare up at the stars. There's about a million of them. You don't see stars like this back home.

I take a swig of my lukewarm Tang and rum. I'm already drunk from the beers I had back at Eddie's, but I don't care. It's weird. I feel reckless, not scared of anything. For once, I'm not worrying about Mom and Will or feeling guilty about Emma.

"Andromeda," Col says suddenly.

I startle. "What?"

"That star, there." He points. "It's actually not a star at all. It's a whole galaxy."

I squint up at a sky so thick with stars that it looks like worn-thin black velvet held over a bright light. "Which one?"

He moves over to sit beside me, lowers his head to my level and points. "See that bright star there? The north star?"

I nod.

"Okay, on one side of it you've got the Big Dipper, right? Look on the other side of it—see Cassiopeia? The W-shaped group of stars?"

I shake my head. "I see the Big Dipper, but..."

"I'll get the binoculars," he says. "You've got to see this. It's incredible."

Col's thigh is warm against mine, and I don't want him to move.

Becca stands up and shakes her blond dreads. "Actually, I've got to go. I'm wiped."

She looks bored, but not particularly tired. I wonder if she's going to go back to Eddie's.

"Rachel? Come on."

Reluctantly, I move away from Col and stand up. I don't want to go back to *Shared Dreams*. I don't want to climb that ladder and lie in my narrow berth high up above the hard parking lot and listen to my mom snoring and Tim muttering in his sleep.

Col's hand brushes my arm, and it feels like a thousand electric shocks. "If you want to stay a bit, I'll show you Andromeda and then run you back to your boat in my dinghy."

I hesitate for a moment. I'm not sure if he's hitting on me or if I'm imagining it. I'm not sure which I want it to be.

"Okay," I say. "That'd be great."

He grins. "Good."

I follow Becca to the stern rail to grab my flashlight and jacket from her dinghy. She steps over the rail, pulls the dinghy close and jumps down lightly.

As I lean over to get my things, she grabs my arm and pulls me close. "Rachel? He's a player, okay? Just so you know."

I nod. "Sure. I'm not staying long. I just don't want to go home yet."

She shrugs. "None of my business what you do. I wouldn't want you to get hurt."

I guess I should be upset that she's saying this, or nervous, or something. But I'm not. I'm excited. Because she wouldn't bother to say it if she didn't think he might be interested.

Ten

Becca pushes her dinghy away from Col's boat and begins rowing.

"Night," I say.

She nods and keeps rowing. I watch her unlit dinghy slipping into the darkness.

Col stands close behind me. Everything feels different now that it's just him and me on the boat. I don't even know him.

"Can I get you another drink?" he asks.

I look at my empty glass swinging from the lifelines in its drink holder. More alcohol is probably not a good idea. On the other hand, what the hell.

"Sure." I follow him down the steps and into the cabin. Even though it's cool out, he's only wearing baggy surf shorts and a white T-shirt. His arms and the back of his neck are darkly tanned and his hair is sun-bleached to a white blond.

Down below, even the dim lights seem too bright, and I'm sure I'm blushing for no reason at all. Col pops open a wooden compartment concealed in the cabin roof and slides out a bottle of wine.

"Special occasion," he says.

I raise my eyebrows, trying to be cool. "Thought you only had rum and Tang."

"Like I said, special occasion."

"Is it?"

His eyes meet mine. They are a dark grayish blue with whites that seem a few shades whiter than most people's.

"Could be," he says. "What do you think?"

I remember Becca saying that he's a player, and I tell myself that it's a totally hokey pick-up line. But I'm nodding my head at the same time. "Why not?" I say.

The thing is, he's in his twenties. He's a pilot, or almost a pilot anyway. He's here on his own boat. From what Becca said, he's got more money that he knows what to do with. And me? I'm sixteen. I get twenty bucks allowance each week. I'm still in high school, and I'm here with my completely screwed-up family. So who am I kidding?

"You still want to see Andromeda?" he asks, pouring two glasses of red wine. Real glasses, not plastic cups.

I take one from him, careful not to let my hand touch his. "Sure."

It's a relief to go back outside, into the darkness. Col sits beside me, close but not quite touching. I'm not sure if I want him to move closer to me or farther away. He lifts the binoculars to his eyes and steadies them, and suddenly I remember Tim doing the same thing that day we saw Mom with Will. My breath catches in my throat, and I try to turn it into a cough.

"You all right?" Col asks, lowering the binoculars and looking at me.

"Fine, sorry." I try to push away thoughts of my mother. "Yeah. Did you—can you see it?"

"Yeah. Here." He hands me the binoculars, but when I take them, he doesn't let go. Instead he moves his hands over top of mine, guiding the binoculars to my eyes so I'm staring through them up at the general vicinity of Andromeda.

I'm not going to see it, I think. I don't really care except that Col obviously wants me to see it and I want to be able to say the right things.

"Okay," he says. "North Star…Cassiopeia…"

"That's the W-shaped one, right?"

"You got it. Now, look just over from there, just above it—you see those three stars in a row?"

I nod, uncertainly. Then I see it: a little patch of light, like a tiny star cloud. A faintly glowing galaxy. "Oh. Oh wow. I see it."

Col sounds pleased. "Isn't it amazing? It blows me away, thinking about it. You know what? That galaxy is two hundred and fifty million light years away. I mean, it could have disappeared millions of years ago and we'd still be seeing it."

I lower the binoculars and stare up at the sky. "It is amazing. Totally amazing."

Col is quiet for a moment. "People always go on about how the stars make them feel so insignificant."

"Uh-huh."

"I think it's the opposite though. I find them reassuring. Like…it's okay if everything doesn't always work out the way you want it to, or if things don't make sense sometimes, because there is so much else out there." He laughs. "God, just listen to me. Sorry, Rachel. Blame it on the wine. I hardly know you, and here I am rattling on about my theory of life."

"It's okay. I—I liked what you said."

"You're sweet."

I laugh. "Well, you're the only one who thinks so."

"What do you mean?"

"Well, let's just say that being stuck on a boat with my parents is not exactly bringing out the sweet side of me."

He raises one eyebrow. I love it when guys do that.

"It's no big deal," I say, shrugging. I wish I hadn't brought up my parents. I don't want to remind him that I'm not here on my own. I take a sip of wine. "This is nice," I say, even though I don't really like the taste of wine at all.

"Australian," he says. "I was down there for a while, a couple of years ago."

"You were?"

"Mmm. Great country."

"When I was a kid, I had this book called *Alexander and the Terrible, Horrible, No Good, Very Bad Day*. It was about this kid who—obviously—is having a bad day and every time a new bad thing happens, he says he's going to move to Australia." God. Why can't I stop making myself sound like a baby?

He doesn't seem to notice though. "Hey, I had that one too. And then at the end, the kid says, 'Some days are like that. Even in Australia.'"

I grin at him. "Yeah." Although actually I don't think it's the kid who says that. I think it's his mom. But I'm through with believing anything mothers say.

He reaches out and touches my hair, his fingers brushing against my cheek for a fraction of a second.

I freeze, barely breathing.

He pulls his hand away. "Your hair's so black," he says. "And you're so fair skinned. Do you dye it?"

"Can't you tell? My roots are totally growing in. I haven't been able to find black hair dye since we left the States." My heart is pounding and my voice sounds funny.

Col touches my hair again and lifts a lock of it teasingly, like he's inspecting the roots. "Don't tell me you're really a blond."

"Yup. 'Fraid so." I make a face. "But only my hair, you know? I've never really felt like a blond."

"Yeah, you don't strike me as the blond type. The black suits you. You're...I don't know. Different."

I watch his face anxiously. Different good or different bad?

"How old are you anyway?" he asks.

I try to remember if I've mentioned that I'm still in school and wonder how big a lie I can get away with. Two years, I decide. I'll add two years. "Eighteen."

Col's eyes narrow to catlike slits when he smiles. "Eighteen, huh?"

I look down at my empty glass. "Yup. Legal drinking age in the Bahamas."

He refills it. "Hmm. But not where you're from, I bet. Are your parents going to kill me?"

"My parents won't find out." I look out across the dark water toward Red Shanks. "Believe me," I say, "I can keep a secret."

Eleven

In a weird way, talking to Col reminds me of talking to Jen. I guess it's just been a long time since I talked to anyone under forty. It's been a long time since I had a conversation about anything other than the boat, the weather and what's for dinner.

"It must be something, traveling with your folks," Col says.

"I didn't want to come," I admit. "But it was okay at first."

I think back to the beginning of the trip. That first day crossing Lake Ontario, long hot August days and warm starry nights, our whole family together on our little boat making our way through the canals and down the Hudson River to New York. It seemed so hopeful. Mom and Dad were actually getting along, and it seemed like things were going to be different.

Tim was in heaven. But I knew it wasn't going to last.

On our first overnight sail on the ocean—off the New Jersey coast—a storm kicked up. The wind sounded like someone screaming, and the boat pounded into the huge dark waves. Spray flew everywhere. Outside, you couldn't see a thing. We were hurtling forward into this awful blackness. When you were down below, it sounded like the boat was being shaken apart. I kept throwing up. I sat outside, shivering and trying to stay under the dodger, listening to Mom and Dad fighting.

Mom screamed at him that he should reef the main sail, that it was too windy, that the boat was out of control, that he was putting their kids in danger.

"Laura," he said in this ultra-calm voice, "I think I know a little more about this than you do."

She pulled her hat off and threw it onto the cockpit floor. "Damn it, Mitch. Stop acting like you're the big expert and I'm just…nothing."

He picked up the hat and wrung water from it. "No one can make you feel inferior without your consent."

"Go to hell," she said. She went down below, and I knew this trip wasn't going to solve one single thing.

Col taps my shoulder. "Hey. Are you okay?"

I shake my head. "I think I better go."

"What is it? What's wrong?"

If I try to talk, I'll start to cry. I stand up and realize that I'm very, very drunk. "I don't know. Nothing. It's just late."

"Did I say something wrong?" His forehead creases with concern. "I asked you about your family. I'm sorry. I didn't mean to make you uncomfortable."

"No, it's okay. It's not your fault." He's so close I can hear his breathing.

He shakes his head. "Look, we can talk about something else. Or we could watch a movie. I got this cute little twelve-volt TV from some cruisers in Luperon last year."

I hesitate, feeling torn. "What time is it?"

Col looks at his watch. "Two."

"I better go. I snuck out, you know? My folks think I'm in bed."

He grins. "Oh yeah. I remember those days." He stands up and holds out a hand. "Okay. I'll run you back to the boatyard on one condition."

"What's that?" I take his hand and he pulls me to my feet.

"You come see me again tomorrow."

I look at him, surprised. "Okay. I…well. Yeah, I'd like that." Since we got back to Georgetown, I've wanted nothing more than to leave. But now I catch myself hoping that the boat won't get fixed too quickly after all.

Col's dinghy is small and wooden. He has an outboard engine, but he doesn't turn it on. Instead, he rows us to shore. The moon is up, and it doesn't seem all that dark anymore. The phosphorescence in the water isn't as bright as it was earlier, but I can still see its milky swirls of light behind the boat.

I bet Emma would have liked to see this, I think.

"Who's Emma?" Col asks.

I realize I must have said the words out loud. "She's my sister. My older sister. She didn't come with us."

"Too bad."

I shrug. "Yeah. She moved out last year."

"I always wished I had a big sister," Col says.

I don't say anything. I know what he's imagining, and it's too hard to explain that it isn't like that with Emma.

When we get to shore, Col jumps out and ties the dinghy to the dock. "I'll walk you back," he says.

"You don't have to."

"Maybe I want to."

"Well. Thanks." I step out of the dinghy and stumble over a piece of wood lying across the dock.

Col grabs my arm and steadies me. "Okay?"

"Sorry, yeah. Fine." I expect him to release my arm, but instead of letting go, he slides his hand down my arm to my hand and grips it tightly. I swallow hard and pretend not to notice that we are holding hands as we walk across the boatyard.

"That's my boat there," I whisper. "I better go."

"Okay." Col releases my hand.

We stand there for a moment, facing each other, and for a crazy second I wonder if he's going to kiss me. Then he steps backward and grins. "See you tomorrow then."

I am as quiet as I can be, climbing up the ladder. In the cockpit, I wait a moment, slipping off my jacket. If I get caught now, I can pretend I just came outside for some fresh air. I listen closely and hear Mom snoring.

Barely breathing, I slip through the companionway, down the steps and into my berth. I lie there, a huge grin on my face, my heart pounding. Col. Col. Col.

"Rach?"

"Tim. Shh."

"Where did you go?" he whispers.

I flip over so my head is at the other end of my berth, closer to Tim's aft cabin. He's kneeling on the end of his bed, shirtless and skinny-chested. "None of your business." But I want to talk about it, so I tell him anyway. "I went to Eddie's and then to visit this guy. Col."

"On a boat?"

"Duh."

He shrugs. "I don't know. He could live here."

"No, he's a cruiser. He's from Palm Beach." I grin smugly, enjoying how the words feel in my mouth. "He's a pilot."

"Cool."

"How come you're awake?"

"I can't sleep." Tim rubs his eyes and even in the dark, I can tell that he's been crying.

"What's wrong?" I feel a flicker of guilt that I've refused to talk to him about what we saw. "Is it…are you thinking about Mom and Will?"

"No. Emma."

"I know. I miss her too."

"I just had a dream about her," Tim says. "About how we used to play Hospital when we were little."

I nod my head. "I remember that. We used to play School too."

"No, we never played School."

"Well, whatever. Those kind of games."

Tim looks at me kind of pityingly, like he can't believe I'm so dumb. "Not whatever. Just Hospital. We used to play it all the time."

"If you say so." I'm pretty sure we played some rocket ship game too.

"We did. And you always made up the rules. You always got to be the doctor, and I always had to be Emma's mom or dad, and Emma...Emma was always the patient."

I haven't thought about this in years, but I can suddenly remember it: the couch turned into a hospital bed, Emma lying on it, me saying, "Lie still, Emma, don't talk, you're supposed to be unconscious."

"I can't believe you remember that," I say.

"I used to like it when you played with me," Tim says. "I remember it." He looks at me for a long second; then he says, "Do you remember that time Mom caught us?"

I shake my head.

"She was so mad," Tim said. "I didn't even know what I'd done wrong."

"Don't be stupid," I said. "You didn't do anything wrong. You were just a little kid."

His eyes catch mine. "I thought you didn't remember."

"Go back to bed," I say. I flip back the other way and pull the pillow over my head. I try to think about Col and recapture that feeling I had a few minutes ago. But it's gone.

I do remember the time Mom caught us playing that game. I must have been about eight; Tim was maybe four. I even remember I was wearing a green dress that I wore practically every day. I loved that dress. God, I haven't thought about this for years, but I remember it like it happened yesterday.

Tim was sitting on the couch with Emma, and I had a skipping rope doubled over and hanging around my neck: my stethoscope. "I'm sorry, Mr. Jones," I told Tim. He was a skinny little kid even then, all ribs and knees and elbows. "I'm afraid your little girl is very badly hurt. She probably won't recover."

And then Mom was running into the room, white-faced, screaming, "What the hell is wrong with you? How could you do this? How could you?" and grabbing Emma off the couch. Emma was giggling; then she burst into tears, and Mom rushed out of the room, carrying her like a baby and making this awful wailing noise.

Tim and I just sat there and stared at each other. Just remembering it, I can feel the hot sick feeling. The guilt. And I remember wondering if she would tell Dad and hoping that she wouldn't.

I roll over on the narrow berth and concentrate on remembering the feeling of my hand in Col's.

Twelve

It feels like about an hour later that Dad is kicking me out of bed.

"Come on, Pookie. Rise and shine."

He hasn't called me that in years. All this sunshine must be cooking his brain. I groan and sit up. "What's the rush?"

Dad flips the folding table down from the wall and starts turning my bedroom back into the living room-kitchen-dining room. "I thought we could all take a little day trip together. We're stuck here anyway, and we'll want to be off the boat while they're working on the rudder."

"Are they starting today then?"

He tousles my hair and grins at me. "Let's hope so."

I don't know what to hope for. I slip out of bed and squeeze past him into the head. In the little green mirror, my eyes are circled with dark smudges. So much for waterproof mascara. I step on the foot pump and splash cold water—the only kind that comes out of our taps—on my face. I feel like I've had about two hours sleep.

My stomach feels like its contents have curdled, and my head is pounding. I rub at the mascara with a wet cloth. Sometimes it's just as well that Dad isn't exactly tuned in.

Back in the cabin, the happy family is gathering around the table for another delicious breakfast of bread, peanut butter and jam. I am so not hungry.

At 8:00 AM sharp, Dad turns on the radio. "Good Morning, Georgetown," Will is saying cheerfully.

I watch Mom's face for any sign of emotion: nervousness, interest, guilt. Nothing.

"Maybe I'll stay on the boat today," I say. "I think I might be coming down with something." If they all go into town, I can call Col on the radio. Maybe he could come and get me.

"It'd be nice to spend the day together," Mom says.

"We spend every day together," I argue. "We've been doing nothing but spending days together."

Mom laughs; then she sighs. "But it's been so busy. Your schoolwork, and all the problems with the boat..."

It's true. It's been one problem after another ever since we left the States. Actually, before that too, but problems were easier to fix back there. We could go to a marina and get a mechanic or whatever. Here in the Bahamas every little stripped screw or lost hose clamp or frayed belt is a huge deal. When we were packing for the trip, I thought we had enough spare parts to practically build a second boat, but somehow we never quite have the parts we need.

"I know," I say. "It's just that I really don't feel that good."

She frowns and puts her hand on my forehead. "You're not hot."

I pull away. "I didn't say I was hot; I said I didn't feel good. Okay? And I don't feel like…like…" I realize that she hasn't actually told me what they were planning for my day.

On the radio, Will is summarizing the weather reports from various sources.

"We thought we could rent bikes and cycle over to Rolletown," Dad says. "Come on, Rachel. It'll be fun."

I shrug. "I went when we were here last time. There's nothing there." It's true, on the surface, but what I don't say is that the view from Rolletown is one of the most beautiful things I've ever seen. I don't say that I walked all the way there the day after we saw Mom kissing Will, or that I tried unsuccessfully to call Jen collect from a phone booth, or that I stood at the top of the Rolletown hill and looked out over the endless water in its thousand shades of blue and cried until I couldn't cry anymore.

Mom and Dad exchange glances.

"I'd really like you to come," Mom says softly.

And I'd really like for you not to fuck around with the neighbors, I think.

Mom sighs. Dad steeples his hands together on the table and for once, says nothing. Tim picks at his fingernails. Actually, his cuticles. He barely has nails left to pick at and the tips of his fingers are all red and swollen and gross-looking. He looks up and catches me staring; then he scowls and tucks his hands under the table.

"I need some time to myself," I say. "I want to write to Jen."

"You could do that later," Mom says.

God. Is a few hours alone really too much to ask? "I'm not going," I say flatly.

Dad shrugs. "Well, it's your choice, I suppose." He fills a water bottle from the tap. "An opportunity missed is an opportunity lost."

I watch them walk across the parking lot. Tim's shoulders are hunched miserably, and I can't help feeling a pang of guilt. I bet he's thinking about Mom and Will all the time and I know I should talk about it with him, but I just can't. If we talk about it, then it really happened. And even though I know it did, I don't want to say it out loud.

As soon as they are out of sight, I turn the radio to channel 16. I push the button to speak. Then I take my thumb off it again. What if he didn't really mean it, about wanting to see me again? What if he was just being polite? I hesitate for a long moment. If I don't call now, god knows when I'll get another chance. I clear my throat and push the button again. "*Flyer, Flyer.* This is *Shared Dreams.*"

Two thoughts occur to me at once: that Col might not even know our boat's name, and that everyone in the anchorage who has their radio turned on just heard me calling him. Shit. What if someone tells my parents? And someone will, guaranteed. You know what people say about small towns and how everyone knows everyone else's business? Well, small towns have nothing on the cruising community.

There's no answer, and I stand there for a moment, undecided. Should I call again? Wait an hour? Maybe he's sleeping in and hasn't turned on his radio yet. Or maybe he's already gone into town, or snorkelling, or something.

In the end, I decide to go into town. Maybe I'll run into him. That might be better anyway, in case he really was just being polite.

I pull on a tight black T-shirt and a pair of dark green surf shorts, run wet hands through my hair, give it a shake and stare at myself in the mirror. I wonder if Col really believed me when I said I was eighteen. Mostly people say I look younger than my age.

I'm climbing down the ladder when a voice startles me.

"Hey there. I didn't realize anyone was still aboard."

A tall black guy who looks a few years older than me is standing beside the boat, his hand resting on the rudder. He's wearing shorts and a T-shirt, and grinning widely.

I nod. "Sorry." I'm not sure why I'm apologizing; I always do that. "I'm just going into town so...uh, there's no one aboard now." Duh. I sound like a total idiot.

"I'll get this sanded down this morning. Try and get the first coat of fibreglass on today."

I'm surprised he's being so friendly, given what a jerk Dad has been. "That's great," I say. "I mean, wonderful. Thanks so much." I'm gushing, being all awkward, being overly friendly. As if I can make up for Dad's behavior. I don't want him to think I'm like that too.

He nods abruptly, suddenly less friendly.

No doubt he thinks I'm a big phony. "Well," I say. "Umm."

"We should have it done in a couple of days," he says.

My heart skips a beat. Before I met Col, there was nothing that would have made me happier than to get out of here. Now I don't want to leave. I don't even care, right now, what Mom does with Will.

I just want to see Col again.

Thirteen

l wander down to the Computer Café to check my e-mail. The computers were all down the last time we were in Georgetown, so I haven't heard from Jen in ages.

Luckily they're working again, though painfully slowly. I run my fingers over the keys, waiting for my inbox to appear, and think about what I'll tell Jen.

I've got mail. Two messages from Jen. I open the most recent one first, sent three days ago. Just a short terse line asking where I am and why I haven't written back. She sounds annoyed, but I've tried to explain before that it isn't always easy. The whole way down the coast, we were anchored miles up these winding rivers in the middle of nowhere. I mean, really nowhere. Tall grassy reeds and crab traps and pelicans. No towns. No Internet cafés. Even when the ICW went through a city, we didn't have a car to get anywhere. And in the Bahamas, the Internet cafés have been pretty few and far between. Most of the islands we've been to don't even have anyone living on them.

Anyway, I don't think she understands. I open her earlier e-mail, from two weeks ago, and read it. *Hey, Rach, So are you still in GT? What's up? I'm seeing this guy I met at a party last weekend. His name's Matt and he's soooo hot. Seriously. School sucks though. We had to do speeches last week. Barf. Mr. Thevin (seven with a lisp) is a pig. Miss u miss u miss u—BFF—Jen.*

It doesn't say much, but it still makes me homesick. I've never been as lonely as I've been these last few months. *Hi Jen,* I type. *I miss you too. I've*...I can't think what to say. I've been bored out of my mind? Mom's screwing around with a guy on another boat? I met this guy but he's like ten years older than me and I don't know if he's interested? In the end, I just write some unimportant stuff. *It's beautiful here, but there's not much to do. Miss hanging out with you. That's cool about you and Matt. Sorry I couldn't reply sooner, but all the computers were down for ages. Done lots of snorkeling and I'm getting a great tan (well, okay—lots of freckles anyway).* Etcetera, etcetera.

After I sign off, I feel kind of depressed. It's always like that. I miss the connection I had with Jen, but whenever I get her e-mails, I feel less connected instead of more. All her stories about going to parties and hanging out at the mall are so hard to relate to from here. It all seems a bit boring, but at the same time I wish I was back there doing that stuff with her.

I sit there for a few minutes, feeling sorry for myself; then I make myself get up and walk over to Exuma Markets. It's a grocery store, but it's also where all the cruisers get their mail. They have a big box with alphabetical files. I check it, but there's nothing for us, so I just buy a postcard and stamps and sit down on a curb outside the store. The sun warms my skin and makes me restless. It feels like someone touching me, and it makes me think of Col. I try to concentrate.

The postcard is for Emma. Hopefully one of the staff will read it to her. *Dear Emma,* I write. *I hope you are having fun and doing lots of great artwork. I miss you a lot. This postcard is a picture of a parrotfish—isn't it beautiful? Maybe you could do a painting of a parrotfish for me to hang on my wall when I get home. The Bahamas are very hot and sunny, and the water is very blue. We are taking lots of pictures to show you when we get home. Lots and lots of love—Rachel*

I'm dropping it in the mailbox when I see Becca walking down the other side of the street, wearing a red bikini top, shorts and sport sandals.

She waves and crosses over the road. "Hey." She looks at me, eyebrows raised. "So?"

"So what?"

"So, what happened last night?"

I shrug. "What do you mean?"

"Come on. With Col."

"Nothing."

She narrows her eyes. "Really? Because I felt kind of bad about leaving you there. I mean, I know what he's like. And you're just a kid."

I can't decide whether to argue with her about me being a kid, or ask what she means about Col. In the end, my need to talk about him wins out. "What do you mean, what he's like?"

She shrugs. "He's all right. Just, you know, what I said last night. He's a player. Lots of girls. Lots."

"I like him."

She looks at me more closely. "Something did happen, didn't it?"

"No, I told you, nothing happened. Honest. He showed me that star, you know, Andromeda. Then he took me home." I suddenly feel kind of flat, because, after all, this is the truth. Nothing did happen. He took me home, and probably he only held my hand because I was drunk and klutzy and he was making sure I got home safely.

Becca relaxes. "Okay. Good. I've been a bit worried all morning, to tell you the truth. He has a bit of a reputation. And you're what—fifteen?"

"Sixteen."

"Yeah."

I have a sudden thought. "Have you and Col...you know...?"

She shakes her head dismissively. "Not a chance. I mean, yeah, he's good looking. But he's a bit too smooth, you know? I'm not into guys like that."

"I thought he seemed nice."

"Oh no. Don't tell me you're falling for him."

"I'm not," I lie. "But he seemed like an okay guy. Maybe whatever you've heard is bullshit, you know?"

"Maybe. But mostly people here seem to know everything about everyone." She shrugs. "People don't have enough to talk about. The gossip's worse than it was in high school."

I wonder if anyone knows about Mom and Will.

"So what are you doing now?" she asks.

"Writing to my friend Jen," I say. "I miss her. I miss my whole life back there. I even miss school." I make a face. "I never thought I'd say that."

"I was supposed to start college last fall," Becca says. "But I grew up around boats, and I learned to sail when I was a kid." She shrugs, as if it's all too complicated and she doesn't want to get into it. "I don't know. Things changed. College didn't seem so appealing. I've been planning this trip since I was your age."

"Wow." I stare at her for a moment. I don't think I've ever really thought very far ahead. I feel like I should have some plans or goals to tell her about, but I really don't. Jen and I never planned much beyond what we'd do the next weekend. I guess university isn't that far off, but beyond trying to get decent grades, I can't say I've given it a lot of thought.

We're still standing there chatting when I see Mom, Dad and Tim cycling slowly down the road. My heart sinks. I thought they'd be gone longer. How am I going to call Col now?

Mom and Tim pull to a stop beside us, and Mom smiles at me. "You should have come, Rachel. The view from Rolletown was amazing."

Dad catches up, out of breath. He's not in such good shape. In fact, since we've been in the Bahamas, he's started to get a beer gut. He nods at me and gives Becca a friendly grin. You'd never guess he suspects her of being a bad influence.

"Hi, Mitch," Becca says. "Are you all coming to the reception at the Peace and Plenty tonight?"

Dad smiles at her, but he looks distracted. "What reception?"

"Tina and Carl's wedding, remember?"

"I'd forgotten." He rubs his hands over his face, which is all sweaty and slightly pink from sunburn and exertion. "Yeah, we'll be there." He turns to Tim and me. "Let's all go back to the boat and get some lunch. And then you two probably better do some schoolwork."

So much for having a day to myself.

The boat feels even smaller and more crowded than usual. Plus, we have to eat lunch to a soundtrack of power sanders and drills. It makes talking difficult, which is fine by me. I don't have anything to say.

Dad seems to think that this noise shouldn't interfere with Tim's or my ability to study, so we sit at the table for a while, staring at our books. All I can think about is how to see Col. I can't call him with my folks on the boat. I guess I could ask to use the dinghy and go over to his boat, but what excuse would I give my parents? Going snorkeling, maybe? But then Tim would have to come with me. We're not allowed to snorkel solo.

Dad keeps poking his head in and checking up on us, so I lie down on the berth and pretend to study. I'm really reading a book of plays: *No Exit*, it's called, by Sartre. It's Tim's. Not the kind of thing I usually read, but it's actually sort of interesting. More interesting than doing the history paper I should be working on. The people in the play are all trapped in this little room together and the idea is that it is actually, literally, hell. I can relate.

Tim gets up and pours himself a cup of water. Then he comes and sits back down at the table. He turns his pages violently and makes these gross noises while he gnaws on his fingers.

"God, Tim. Can't you go outside or something?"

He looks at me and blinks.

Suddenly I can't stand it anymore. Tim, my parents, this boat, this whole stupid fucking trip. I want to scream.

I take a deep breath and glare at Tim. "You're in my personal space."

He blinks again. "Where exactly do you want me to go?" he says slowly. Then he glares at me. "Hey, that's my book."

"Have you read it?"

"Sure. Of course."

I scowl. "You know what Sartre said?"

He shrugs. "He was a philosopher. He said lots of things."

"He said, *Hell is other people*. And you know what? He was so fucking right." I toss the book at him, stand up and climb the companionway steps, and walk past Mom and Dad in the cockpit.

"I can't concentrate with this noise," I say. "I'm going for a walk."

Dad says something, but I tune him out. I can't stand being on this boat for another second. I climb down the ladder.

"Be back by five," Mom calls after me. "We've got that thing to go to at the Peace and Plenty this evening."

"I'll meet you there," I say as I walk away.

Fourteen

I walk back into town, kicking my feet at the dry sandy dirt along the edge of the road. I hope Becca is still around. If I don't talk to someone, I think I might explode.

But I can't see her anywhere. I walk the loop of road, check the Two Turtles patio and shops and the library. She might have gone back to her boat. In the end, I just walk around all afternoon, thinking. I can't stop thinking. There's not much point trying to make sense of what Mom did, or of why my family seems to be falling apart. Even if I could figure out what went wrong, I couldn't change anything. Still, I can't stop going around in the same stupid circles.

Finally I buy a skinny blue notebook and a cheap pen at Exuma Market and sit down under a bare-branched tree. Maybe if I write it down, I can get it out of my head. Dad used to get me to do this when I was a kid and stuff was bothering me, but I haven't done it in years.

Why everything is so fucked up, I write.

1. *Mom and Dad...I don't know. Growing apart? Total cliché.*
2. *While we're on clichés, how about mid-life crisis? Maybe that's what Mom was doing with Will. Having a mid-life crisis. It sure looked like kissing though. It sure looked like cheating on Dad.*
3. *Family time. I don't get it. Mom and Dad barely talk for months and then all of a sudden it's Family Dinners, Family Mission Statements, Family Game Nights. What the hell could have made them think this trip was a good idea?*
4. *Emma?*

I stop writing. Emma's accident, Emma moving out. Was that what everything came back to? Maybe Emma had been the only thing holding us together. Maybe she was the glue. I stare at the page for a moment. Fuck it. I don't know the answers. I tear the page out, rip it up and stuff the pieces in my shorts' pocket. I won't think about it. There's no point.

I stare at the blank page and let my mind drift. After a few minutes I pick up my pen again and write *Col. Col. Colton. Flyer.* I trace the words with my fingertip. The sun is hot and silky against my skin. I wrap my arms around my knees, close my eyes and wonder if it's possible to get high from the sunlight and my own thoughts.

At five thirty, I wander over to the Peace and Plenty Hotel. It's a pink building, kind of fancy compared with anywhere else here, but not so fancy that I'm worried about showing up for a wedding reception in shorts and a T-shirt. Mom won't appreciate it, but I'm sure I won't be the only one. It's not like anyone has formal wear stowed on their boat. Mostly I'm hoping there's some food happening. I'm starving.

The reception is on the patio area around the swimming pool. It's the tiniest pool, but it seems odd to have a pool at all when you're surrounded by clear blue sea. I'm not late, but a lot of people are already here. They're buzzing around the food table like flies. The newlyweds are there, of course. Tina's wearing a long, pale blue dress, and Carl's wearing cream-colored pants and a button-down shirt. I guess that's casual for your own wedding reception, but it's the most dressed up I've seen anyone in a while.

I nod and smile at them. Tina waves back. I'm not sure if I should go and say hi or anything. I don't know them that well. They're my parents' age, and I imagine they've both been married before. Their boat is called *Cat's Meow*, and they're from Toronto. I've noticed that a lot of the Canadians here act like they're all old friends, even if they have nothing else in common. That's probably why we were invited. Although, looking around, it looks like just about everyone was.

I'm standing there feeling awkward when my parents arrive, right on time. It's one thing they do have in common

I guess—they both hate being late. Tim is walking between them as usual, stiff-looking in a long-sleeved shirt that I didn't know he'd brought.

"Hey," he says to me. "Have you checked out the food? I'm starving."

Mom and Dad wander off to mingle, and Tim and I head for the food table.

"You'll never guess what happened this afternoon," he says.

"Um, let me think. Nothing?"

He makes a face. "Ha ha. No, seriously. Some guy had a heart attack over on Volleyball Beach."

"Really? Who?"

"Not anyone we know. A guy from South Africa."

"Wow. Was he…is he okay?"

Tim shrugs. "No one knows. I guess he sort of collapsed during the volleyball game and some people did CPR. And then they got him on a plane to Nassau, to go to the hospital there."

"Wow. That sucks."

"I know." He piles conch fritters onto a plate. "Dad said it just goes to show."

"Show what?" I ask, instantly feeling irritated.

"You know. That you don't know what the future holds. So, 'gather ye rosebuds while ye may.'"

My brother, the freak. "'Gather ye rosebuds'? What the hell are you talking about?"

"You know, *Carpe Diem.*" Tim pops a fritter into his mouth without looking up at me. "Hey, there's your friend."

For a heart-stopping second I think he means Col. But of course, he hasn't even met him. I turn and see Becca approaching.

"Oh. Hi. I was looking for you this afternoon," I tell her.

She grins. "I went spear fishing. It was so cool."

"Seriously?"

"Yeah. I got a grouper. And the guys I went with caught two lobsters." She grabs a plate and starts helping herself from an enormous bowl of macaroni and cheese. "So why were you looking for me?"

I hesitate, glance at Tim, and then look back at Becca. "Nothing major. I'll tell you later."

Tim piles a slice of tomato on top his mountain of food. "Don't let me interfere. I'm going to talk to Mango anyway." He turns away, carefully balancing his plate as he weaves through the crowd.

Becca looks concerned. "What is it, Rachel? Is everything okay?"

I feel an awful wave of self-pity and try to shrug it off. "It's just a bit hard, sometimes, being here with my family. And, I don't know. I miss my sister." I stare at my plate. Conch, grouper, lettuce and tomato swim before me, and I blink back the tears. "I'm sorry. I don't want to dump all this on you."

She starts to say something; then she breaks off. "Parent alert. Yours are headed this way." She touches my arm briefly. "Look, I'll make sure we get a chance to talk, okay?"

I nod gratefully. I don't know how much I want to say, but if I don't talk to someone about at least some of this stuff, I'll go nuts.

Becca dumps a huge scoop of macaroni and cheese on my plate. "Eat up."

"Thanks," I say. "Thanks."

My parents have found a table and beckon to me to join them.

Mom's hair is tied up in a knot, with loose curls spilling out around her face. She's not wearing makeup or anything, but she looks good. She's so tall that even in a faded denim skirt and a slightly wrinkled sleeveless top, she looks like she's modeling an outfit for a fashion magazine. She smiles at Becca. "Why don't you sit with us too, Rebecca? If you don't already have a table."

I expect Becca to make some excuse, but to my surprise she says, "Thanks," and sits down. I take a bite of mac and cheese and practically choke as the two empty chairs at our table are filled by Will and Sheila. I can't sit here and make small talk with him. I can't do it. I look around a little wildly. I guess I could go to the washroom, but I'd just have to come back again. I'm trapped.

Will flashes me a big clueless grin. I notice that he has some food stuck to his front teeth. Gross.

"So how's Rachel?" he says.

I shove a huge conch fritter in my mouth and shrug apologetically.

Becca comes to my rescue. "So the rudder repair's going well?" she asks my mom.

Mom looks surprised, probably because for some sexist reason people usually only ask my dad about the boat. "Oh, well, I think it's going well. They were working on it today."

"Yeah, I heard. I went fishing with Terry—you know, from the boatyard—this afternoon, and he said he'd got the first coat of fibreglass on a rudder repair and might as well do some fishing while it dried. I figured that it was your boat he was talking about." Becca smiles at my mother. "Are you going to head back out then? On to the Turks and Caicos?"

Mom hesitates. "We're taking it one step at a time."

This is news to me. "You mean we might stay here longer?" I blurt out.

Will slaps his leg and grins widely at my mother. "That's wonderful news," he says. "I'd sure love to see you stay a little longer."

I bet you would, I think. I just bet you would.

Mom shifts in her seat and changes the subject. "Where's your brother?"

"I don't know. Around." I keep my eyes on my mother and avoid looking at Will. "I think he went to talk to Mango."

Dad frowns. He looks tired. The lines in his forehead and around his mouth are deeply etched. All frown lines, no laugh lines. He's always so serious about everything. Kind of like Tim. "I don't know why a man that age would want to hang around with a twelve-year-old." He clears his throat. "It makes me more than a little uncomfortable."

"Mango's a good guy," Becca says easily. "I don't think you need to worry."

I nod. "He and Tim read all the same stuff. Seriously, I think Tim has more in common with Mango than he had with any of his friends back home."

Dad stands up and looks around. "I can't see him."

"I don't blame you for being concerned," Will says. "The man is definitely strange. I certainly wouldn't trust him."

I snap. "*You're* telling my dad who he should trust?"

There is an awful silence. A terrible silence. My mouth is dry as sand, and no words will come. Everyone is staring at me.

Fifteen

It is Becca, who has no idea what is going on, who comes to my rescue.

"I think Rachel's a bit upset because Mango is a good friend of ours," she says. "Mitch, I can totally understand where you're coming from because Tim's your kid. I mean, it's your job to protect him." She gives him her easy smile. "But honestly, Rachel's right. Mango is the last person you need to worry about."

Dad sits back down slowly and looks at me. "I didn't realize you knew him so well."

I don't, really. But Becca has thrown me a lifeline, and I'm clinging to it. I nod, eyes on my plate. "Yeah," I whisper. "He's a good guy."

Dad seems like he might have forgotten about my rudeness to Will. I slowly look up and flick my eyes around the table, quickly taking in all the expressions. Dad's jaw is still clenched, but he's calming down. Sheila's lipsticked mouth is open in bewilderment. Will is red-faced and angry. And Mom? She's staring at me, and she's gone completely white.

I wonder how much I have given away. She must guess that I know something. Or maybe she's just shocked by my rudeness.

Becca smoothly changes the subject, somehow managing to get everyone talking about the heart-attack guy on Volleyball Beach. I just sit there for a few minutes, not hearing a word of the conversation. I can't believe what I almost did.

Finally Becca grabs my arm. "I'm going up for dessert," she says. "Come with me."

I've barely eaten anything on my plate, but I stand up and numbly follow her across the patio. She steers me past the buffet table, past the washrooms, away from the crowds and into a little alcove in the side wall of the building.

"Okay, Rachel." She looks at me hard. "Do you want to tell me what is going on?"

I shake my head helplessly. I do want to, but if I talk, I'll start crying. My throat aches from holding back tears.

"Come on. Spill it. What's wrong?"

"Can I stay on your boat tonight?" I blurt out. "Please?" I push my fists against my eyes for a few seconds. "Fuck. I'm sorry. I don't want to do this."

Becca grabs me and gives me a hug and that does it: I start crying like a baby, in great shuddering gulps. It's a relief, in a way. We just stand there like that for a couple of minutes, me leaning against her with my head on her shoulder.

Finally, I run out of tears and pull away. "I'm sorry. I don't usually, you know..." I wipe my face with my T-shirt. "I bet I look awful."

"You look fine," Becca says. She is frowning: two vertical lines forming deep creases between her eyebrows. "You're welcome to stay on my boat if your parents will let you."

"They probably won't," I say despairingly. I can't stand the thought of going back to *Shared Dreams* with them tonight. I don't want Mom to know that I know about Will. I don't want her to admit it.

"Rachel...did Will do something to you? Was that what you meant?"

Her voice is low and serious, and for a second I wonder what would happen if I said yes.

I shake my head. "Not exactly. I can't tell you. But please...if I could come to your boat..."

Becca nods. "How about I go talk to your parents for a few minutes and see what I can do, okay? I can be pretty persuasive."

"Should I come?"

"No, just stay here, and I'll be back."

Becca is gone for what seems like ages. I sit in my little alcove, legs folded underneath me on the warm concrete. I don't know if Mom and Dad will agree, but just the possibility makes me feel a little better. It occurs to me that if I stay on Becca's boat, I could call Col. I remember the feeling of his hand in mine and that moment when we were saying good night and I thought he might kiss me. It was only last night, but it feels like days ago.

When Becca returns, she has a wide grin on her face. "They said yes?"

"They did. You can stay with me tonight, but they want you home by dinnertime tomorrow." She raises her eyebrows. "Impressed? You going to ask me how I did it?"

I am impressed. Staying out until dinnertime means she got me out of an afternoon of schoolwork too. "How did you do it?" I ask obediently.

"Well...I told them you were having a hard time. I said you were really homesick and finding it hard not having friends your own age."

"All true," I mumble.

"And your dad went into a long spiel about adolescents and peer relationships—hey, how come you never told me he was a kiddie shrink?"

I shrug. "You never asked."

"Anyway, I listened and agreed with everything he said." She laughed. "I said how lucky you were to have a father with that background—that he obviously really understood what you were going through."

I pretend to gag.

"I know, I know. It was a bit over the top. But it worked anyway. You're staying at my place tonight."

"Thanks. I can't tell you how much I appreciate it."

"It's no big deal." She looks at me curiously. "I know you have a hard time with your dad, but, to tell you the truth, he actually seems like a pretty good guy to me."

"I guess you didn't get any of his inspirational speeches," I say.

"Actually, I got the one about hard times making us stronger in the long run. I remember that one from my grandmother." Becca laughs. "Oh, and he quoted Lord Byron too: 'Adversity is the path to truth.'"

Truth. Whatever that might be. I shrug, feeling tired. "Well, thanks."

"No problem. Like I said, he was pretty nice about it all. He obviously wants you to be happy."

"You think? Then why doesn't he ever listen to me? How come he's been too busy with his screwed-up clients to even notice that his own kids have moved on from kindergarten? I mean, he didn't even bother coming to my grade nine grad."

Becca looks uncomfortable. "Look, I didn't mean to hit a nerve."

I stand up. "It's okay. Just, nothing is what it seems, you know? Nothing is what it looks like from the outside."

"Ain't that the truth," Becca says.

Sixteen

Becca's boat, Sister Ocean, is small and sleek: a narrow-hulled twenty-six-foot Contessa with a dark blue hull. She's anchored in Red Shanks, like we were before we got hauled out. I'm tooth-chattering cold by the time we arrive—it's cold and dark, and all I have on is my T-shirt and shorts.

Becca ties her dinghy to a stern cleat, and we scramble aboard.

"I forgot," she says. "Terry's coming around tonight."

"Terry?"

"Yeah. From the boatyard, you know? The guy who's fixing your rudder."

I think back to this morning. "The really tall guy?"

She laughs. "Yeah. That's him."

"So…I mean, is it going to be okay that I'm here?"

Becca unlocks the companionway hatch and slides the wooden boards out. "Yeah, don't worry. It's fine." She steps inside and beckons to me. "Come on in."

It's pretty basic down below: none of the clutter of *Shared Dreams* and none of the tidy coziness of *Flyer*. I'm short enough to stand up inside, but Becca's head brushes the cabin roof. It's all smooth varnished wood except for the narrow blue cushions on the berths. A sleeping bag and a book are tossed up in the V-berth, where Becca obviously sleeps, and a few faded photographs are neatly taped above a tiny navigation table.

"What do you think?" she asks.

"It's great," I say.

"There aren't many boats this small that are seaworthy enough to cross oceans," she says. "I'd trust this one with my life."

I nod. "Do you mind if I ask you…well, you said you'd been planning this trip for years, right?"

"Right."

"But you're only nineteen. How did you afford to do this? If you don't mind me asking."

Becca shakes her head. "It's okay. Everyone asks that question. My dad died when I was fifteen and left me quite a lot of money. I mean, not like millions or anything, but enough to buy a boat and put off going to college for a couple of years."

"Jeez. I'm sorry. I mean, about your dad." I wrap my arms around myself and wonder if Becca would lend me a sweatshirt.

"Yeah. It sucked."

I wonder what it would be like not to have a father. No family mission statements, no schedules, no inspirational speeches. Much as I hate all that stuff, trying to imagine life without my father makes me feel sort of dizzy and disoriented. I shiver and hug myself tighter. "How did he die?"

"Car accident. He was drunk. As he was most nights."

"Jeez." I sit down on the starboard berth. "I'm sorry."

"Yeah. I was pretty messed up for a while there." Becca shrugs. "I saw one of those kiddie shrinks, like your dad, you know? He really helped a lot. Plus I went to Al-Anon, which was good too."

"Wow. I didn't know that. You always seem so... together."

Becca notices that I'm shivering and lifts a sweater out of a locker under the port berth. "Yeah. Like you said, nothing is what it looks like from the outside."

"Thanks." I take the sweater from her and pull it over my head. It's made of rough blue wool that feels scratchy against my neck. The sleeves are about a foot longer than my arms.

"Rachel? Can I say something without you getting mad?"

"What is it?"

She hesitates for a moment, like she's choosing her words carefully. "Well, my dad had his problems, but I'd give anything to have him back." She sits down across from me. The boat is so narrow, our knees almost touch. "I know you're pissed off at your father, but at least he's trying to be there, you know?"

My eyes are stinging. "Bit late."

"Maybe. But not that many guys would take a year away from their jobs to go traveling with their family. Couldn't you..." She breaks off and grimaces apologetically. "I don't know, just give him a chance?"

"He practically ignored me and Tim until this year," I say gruffly. "That doesn't just get wiped out because he has a mid-life crisis and decides he wants to get to know us. It doesn't work like that."

"No, I know."

This whole conversation is making my stomach hurt. I don't want to talk about my dad anymore. "So...anyway. What time is Terry coming?"

She glances at her watch. "It's seven now. Anytime, I guess. Do you want something to drink?"

"Sure." I roll up my sleeves and watch while Becca pours two glasses of water and stirs in a scoop of orange powder. Tang. It's the only way to make the brackish town water here taste okay. Awhile back, Dad started adding bleach to our water tanks and now our water not only tastes slightly salty, it also smells like a swimming pool.

"Hey, Becca? I told Col last night I'd come see him again. You think I could give him a call?"

She spins around. "I knew it. You so have a crush on him. Admit it."

I groan. "Okay, okay. I guess I do, a little."

She shakes her head. "Be careful, okay? Remember what I told you about him."

"I know. I just want to see him, that's all. And I can't

even call him from my own boat because there is never a moment's privacy."

She passes me a handheld VHF radio. "All yours."

I feel shy calling him and even shyer because Becca is standing there watching. "Thanks." I press the button and call, "*Flyer, Flyer,* this is *Sister Ocean.*"

Col's voice answers almost immediately. "Becca? Try seventy-two, then up one."

I switch to 72, but it is being used by a woman passing on a recipe for conch curry, so I go up one channel to 73. "*Flyer,* this is *Sister Ocean.* Over."

"*Sister Ocean, Flyer* here. Over."

"It's Rachel, though. I'm on Becca's boat. Over."

There's a moment's pause before he replies. "Rachel! That's great. I was starting to think I wasn't going to hear from you. Over."

"It was kind of a crazy day. What are you up to? Over."

"Not much. Want to come hang out? I could pick you up. Over."

My heart leaps. Yes, yes, yes. I'm about to reply when Becca puts her hand on my arm and shakes her head. "I told your parents that I'd take care of you," she says. "I'm not covering for you while you spend the night with Col."

"I wouldn't do that," I say defensively. "I just want to see him."

"Well, you can do that here. Invite him over."

It's better than nothing, though maybe not a lot better if Becca is going to start acting like my parents and monitoring my every move.

"*Sister Ocean*, you still there? Over."

"Yes. Sorry. Look, Becca says why don't you come over here and hang out? Over."

"Sounds good," Col says. "I'll see you soon. Over."

I wonder if he's at all disappointed that we won't be alone together.

If I'd been thinking clearly, I would have stopped off at the boatyard to get my things from *Shared Dreams* before coming over here. As it was, I'd just wanted to get away as fast as possible. Becca takes pity on me and lets me borrow some eyeliner and even finds me a spare toothbrush to use. At least her boat has a decent mirror.

I study my reflection and wonder what it would be like if Col kissed me. I've had boyfriends before, but they were nothing like him. The last one was at the beginning of grade ten: Paul McCoy, my chemistry lab partner. We used to go for walks at lunch and hold hands, and sometimes at parties we'd make out. He always shoved his tongue in my mouth, and I always wondered what the big deal was. We didn't go very far. I mean, he touched my breasts but not under my clothes. He used to squeeze them like he was trying to figure out if they were ripe or not. I wanted to have a boyfriend, but I didn't really like Paul touching me.

I slip off Becca's sweater, lift up my T-shirt and look down at myself. My bra is very white against the freckled skin of my chest and shoulders. I unsnap the front clasp and study my breasts. They are small, and against my sort-of-tan they look almost as white as the bra. It's strange to think that someone might want to touch them.

I don't think I'd mind if Col wanted to.

Terry arrives before Col. We hear his engine approaching; then his dinghy bumps against the hull. Becca leaps up and goes up to the cockpit to welcome him aboard. I can hear them whispering outside for a minute or two before they climb down the steep stairs into the cabin.

"Hi," Terry says. "You're the one from the boat in the yard, right? With the cracked rudder?"

I nod. "Yeah. Rachel."

He ducks his head—he has to hunch way over in Becca's little boat—and shakes my hand. "Good to meet you again."

Becca puts on some music, and she and Terry chat about fishing. My family hasn't done any fishing on this trip, though I remember Dad buying some fishing gear before we left. It sounds like Becca does a lot though, and she keeps asking Terry questions about what kind of reef fish are safe to eat.

"I read that you can cook barracuda with a silver coin inside," Becca says. "If the coin turns black, the fish is contaminated."

Terry laughs. "Nah. That's an old story, but I wouldn't count on it." He folds his legs underneath him on the berth. "I've had ciguatera poisoning once, and it's no fun at all. I was sick for months. I couldn't walk a straight line. I'd take a sip of beer, and it'd taste hotter than coffee. It's the weirdest thing."

"Too bad," Becca said. "Barracuda are so damn easy to catch. I'm always tossing them back in, and it seems such a waste."

There's a lull in the conversation, and I ask Terry something I've been wondering about. "What's it like to live here? I mean, it's beautiful, but it's so isolated."

"Isolated? From what?"

I shrug. "I don't know. Cities, I guess. Just—being on a little island with water all around."

He laughs. "I can hop on a plane and be in Nassau in an hour."

"I guess so."

Becca looks at me. "Terry went to university in New York," she says.

I try not to look surprised. "You did? So why…?"

"Why am I back here working at the dockyard?" He laughs again, his eyes crinkling. "I like it here. And there aren't a lot of jobs for graphic artists, though I do what I can."

"Terry does website design," Becca explains.

I feel oddly disconcerted. I've been so angry with Dad for his attitude and assumptions about the Bahamians, but I'm not much better.

"Ahoy, *Sister Ocean*," a voice calls.

"That's Col," I say. I'm not sure whether I should go

and greet him, since I called him, or whether Becca will, since it's her boat.

Becca grins at me. "If you two want to sit out in the cockpit and chat, we won't be offended."

"Thanks," I say, surprised. Then I notice how close Terry is sitting to her, and the way she keeps looking at him, and I realize that she's the one who wants some privacy.

Col climbs aboard. "Hey."

"Hey," I say.

It's a dark night. The moon has slipped behind the clouds and the wind is picking up, clanking the halyards against the mast and rippling the water even here in the protection of Red Shanks.

"It must be getting rough in Kidd Cove," I say.

Col nods. "Looks like another cold front is moving through."

We stand there awkwardly for a moment. "Becca has a friend over," I tell him. "We can go down below if you want, or we can sit out here."

"This is cool," he says. "I'd rather be outside anyway. Want to go up to the foredeck where we can really feel the wind? Or will you be too cold?"

I glance down through the open companionway and see Terry and Becca down below. She's snuggled up beside him, her head on his shoulder. He's talking, but I can't hear what he's saying over the wind and the music drifting out of the cabin.

"I like the foredeck," I say. "It's my favorite place on my boat. It's the only place where I can get any privacy." I blush. "I mean, you know. From my family."

Col follows me up to the foredeck. We sit side by side, our backs against the hard white fibreglass of the cabin roof. It's a tiny spot we're sharing, and our hips and shoulders touch lightly. Around us, the anchorage is still and dark, the outlines of the islands black against the sky. A few anchor lights glow dimly on distant boats. The wind whips my hair straight back and fills me with a wild, reckless excitement. "I love this weather," I say. "You know, I didn't even want to come on this trip."

"You didn't? How come?"

I wrap my arms around myself and tuck my hands inside the long sleeves of Becca's sweater. "Didn't want to leave my friends or miss school." I remember I've told him I'm eighteen. I keep talking, hoping he'll just assume I meant college. "I don't always get along so well with my folks and being stuck on a boat...well, you can imagine."

He nods. "Yeah, that's why I travel solo. Living on a boat can put a real strain on any relationship." He looks at me and his face is only inches from mine. "It gets kind of lonely though, sometimes."

I swallow hard and am glad of the darkness. "I guess it would."

"So what are your parents like? Had they done much sailing before this?" he asks.

I shrug. "Before this trip, Dad was always working. He sailed on weekends, some. But this is something he's always wanted to do."

"And your mom?"

"I don't think she was so into it, but you know parents. They always have to pretend to agree on stuff even when it's obvious they don't."

Col laughs. "You think? Mine sure didn't." He sticks his hand in his pockets. "They didn't bother to pretend, I mean. It might have been more peaceful if they had."

"I hate pretending," I say. "I hate lies. I hate it when everyone acts like everything is okay when it's not okay at all."

"Whoa." He leans back and looks at me. "I just meant that sometimes going along to get along is better than fighting all the time."

I picture Mom in Will's arms. "It's dishonest," I say. "If people really don't agree, why do they stay together?"

Col shrugs. "Lots of reasons, I guess. People are pretty complicated." He pulls a small plastic bag from his pocket and shows it to me. "I didn't know if you smoked, but I got this from a guy back at Norman's Cay. It's pretty good."

I've never smoked pot before, but I don't really want to say that. "Umm. Not much. I mean, I've tried it, but..."

He pulls a skinny joint out of the bag. "Well, we'll just smoke a little. It'll keep us warm anyway." He pulls his knees up in front of him and cups his hands, trying to shelter the cigarette lighter for long enough to get the joint lit. He's wearing shorts, and his legs are tanned a smooth dark brown against the whiteness of the deck.

I wonder what would happen if I touched him. If I just reached out and put my hand on his thigh. The hair on his leg looks soft as silk. I look away and suddenly wish we were in a house somewhere, and I could run into another room and call Jen on my cell.

I know what she'd say. She'd tell me to go for it.

Seventeen

I take a few cautious drags on the joint. It's okay. I kind of like the smell, but nothing much happens, which is actually a bit of a relief.

Col leans back and closes his eyes, and in the same movement he stretches one arm out behind him and drapes it across my shoulders. It's so casual, like he's just put his arm there by mistake, or because it's a comfortable position.

I can barely breathe.

"So," I say, "how long are you going to be cruising for? I mean, do you have to go back the States in the spring?"

He keeps his eyes closed, and I watch his face while he talks.

"I'll go back for a while. Hang out at my parents' place in the Hamptons and catch up with some friends there," he says. "I'll probably fly back though. Leave the boat here."

"Oh."

There is a long, long silence. I don't know what else to say. I can't say much about my life back home because I

don't want him to ask if I'm in college or whatever, and I
don't want to talk about my family. And I'd like to ask him
more questions, but I don't want him to think I'm being
too nosy. So I just sit and listen to the wind in the rigging
and watch the dark sky and the clouds rolling across the
moon. No stars tonight.

He opens his eyes and turns toward me. "How are you
feeling?"

"Good." I manage to look him right in the eyes. His are
gray and clear and make me feel dizzy. Or maybe that's the
pot, I don't know.

"Good," he says. "Me too."

Then he pulls me toward him and his hand is on the
back of my neck and his lips are on mine, and it's nothing
like kissing Paul McCoy. Nothing at all.

I don't know how much time has passed when it starts to
rain. Ten minutes? Twenty? An hour? We're lying on the
deck, and Col is sort of beside me and sort of on top of
me. One of his hands is under my shirt, touching me, cool
against my skin. I ignore the first drops of rain that fall on
my face and bare legs.

Col slips his hand out from under my shirt and places
it on the inside of my knee, then runs it slowly up my
thigh. I watch his face. His eyes are half closed. When his
hand slides inside the loose fitting leg of my shorts, I catch
my breath with a gasp and then pull away.

"Col, stop." When I try to sit up, I feel dizzy and disoriented. "We'd better…it's raining."

"Rachel…" He lifts himself off me and kneels there for a moment. "God. Come back to my boat with me."

I shake my head. "I can't. I mean, my parents would freak out, and Becca won't cover for me."

Col lets out a long slow breath. "Okay. You're right." He shakes his head. "We shouldn't be doing this anyway. You're so young."

"I'm eighteen," I say quickly. "That's not so young. Anyway, you should come inside and hang out for a bit. At least until it stops raining."

He shrugs. "Sure. The rain here never lasts more than a few minutes."

It is weird to feel disconnected after being so close. I snuggle up to him again, burrow my head against his chest. "Col?"

He wraps his arms around me tightly. "Mmm?"

"I didn't really want you to stop. You know?"

He laughs and strokes my hair. "Me neither." Then he pulls me to my feet. "Come on. You're getting soaked."

Down in the cabin, Becca and Terry are playing cards. It's warm and bright and the music is playing softly.

"It's raining," I say.

Becca laughs. "Yeah, we were wondering if you two were ever going to come inside."

I peel off my wet sweater. "Sorry. Your sweater…"

"Just hang it on the back of the door to the head. I'll grab you something dry to put on."

She finds me a pair of flannel pants and a gray hoodie, and I take the soft bundle into the head to change.

The girl who looks back at me from the mirror is a different girl than the one I saw earlier. My hair is a wild wet tangle of black streaked with blue, my eyeliner is smudged darkly around my eyes, and my lips are swollen from kissing. And I can't stop smiling, even when I try. I feel like laughing out loud.

Terry and Col both leave when the rain stops a few minutes later. Becca and I stand in the cockpit, shivering, and wave good-bye. Then we climb back down below.

"So?" Becca asks.

I just grin. "What?"

"Oh, boy. You've got it bad, don't you?"

I shrug and try to keep my grin to a more reasonable width. "Umm. Maybe." I change the subject. "What about you and Terry? I didn't know you were seeing him."

"We've been hanging out for a couple months," she says.

"Huh. That's cool."

"Don't change the subject," she says. "We were talking about you and lover boy. What were you two getting up to out there in the rain?"

"Just talking," I say. And then, because really I am dying to talk about this and Jen isn't here, I add, "and kissing too."

"Uh-huh. I figured. And that's it?"

I nod. "This is kind of embarrassing but I've never, you know, really done more than that."

"Why's that embarrassing?"

"I don't know. It just is."

She lifts a stack of blankets out of a locker and starts making up a bed for me on one of the berths. "It shouldn't be. I don't want to sound like your mother or something, but your first time should be with someone special. Someone you really care about."

"Believe me, you don't sound like my mother. This is not something we talk about." I picture my mom in Will's arms again and feel a flash of anger. "And I wouldn't take advice from her anyway."

She smoothes down the sheet and tucks the corners under the cushion, and then shakes a blanket out over top. "Your mom seems so nice, Rach. She's always so friendly. And when I talked to your folks tonight, it was obvious that she's really worried about you."

A bottle of wine is sitting open in the galley sink. "Can I have a drink of that?"

"Sure." Becca pours me a glass. She sits down beside me on the berth and hands it to me. She hesitates for a moment before speaking. "Rachel...are you sure you don't want to tell me what is going on?"

I take a gulp of wine and feel its warmth spread

through me. "I do want to tell you. I really want to tell someone. I just…I probably shouldn't."

"Why not?"

"It's not just about me. And I don't want anyone else to know."

Becca's eyes are steady on mine. "I can keep a secret."

"I don't know." I wonder if I would tell Jen, if she were here. I don't know who I can trust with this.

"I don't want to push you," Becca says. "I just want you to know that if you want to talk, it's okay."

Tears are welling up in my eyes and I rub my sleeve across them. "Quit being so nice," I say. "Look what you're doing to me."

She laughs. "Let's go to bed, hey? It's late."

I nod, drink the last of my wine and get into the bed she has made for me. "Thanks, Becca."

She's climbing into the V-berth. "Aren't you going to brush your teeth?"

I groan. "No, Mom."

She laughs again. "Okay, okay. Sorry."

"S'all right." I roll over on the narrow berth. "I'm kidding."

"Night, Rachel."

"Night." I lie still, curled on my side. I close my eyes and imagine that Col is lying behind me, curled around me, holding me close to him. I imagine that I can hear his breathing and feel the beat of his heart. I'm tired of always feeling so alone.

Eighteen

In the morning, Becca makes us scrambled eggs while we listen to the Georgetown morning show. Another cold front, another volleyball game, another Christian Fellowship meeting. Will's thought for the day is this: *The truth will set you free, but first it will give you a really bad day.*

I can't help letting out a disgusted snort. The truth would do a lot more than just give him a bad day.

Becca laughs and scoops mounds of eggs onto two plates. "I thought it was kind of funny."

"I can't stand that guy," I say.

"Mmm. I've noticed. You sure you don't want to tell me what it's all about?" She pushes one plate over to me and sits down across the table.

I poke the eggs with my fork. "I do want to." I think about it for a minute. I didn't want to last night. But I trust Becca. I don't think she'd tell anyone else. It's just that whenever I think about what happened, what Tim and I saw, I feel this awful sense of shame. But it's not my fault that we saw her. It's not my fault that she was kissing Will.

"Then tell me." Becca slides her plate to one side, puts her elbows on the table and leans toward me. "Come on. It's not good to carry stuff around on your own like this."

I nod. "I know. I just…it's hard. Promise you won't tell anyone?"

She nods.

I try to think of the right words. "Will…I think…no, I know…he and my Mom were…" I can't say it.

Becca's eyes open wide. "What? They were involved or something?"

Involved. "That's one way of putting it," I say.

"You mean here? I mean, not like they knew each other back in high school or something?"

I nod. "Here. Last week."

"How do you know?"

"I saw them. Tim and I did. He was…well, Sheila's always nude sunbathing, and I guess he was trying to get a look. He had the binoculars…"

"Holy shit," Becca says. "Holy shit. So what did you see?"

I glare at her. "We saw enough."

"Hey, relax. I wasn't being nosy. I wondered if…well, could you have misinterpreted it?"

I shake my head. "Not a chance. They were kissing. Like, full-on kissing. He was naked. And he had his hand on her ass." I realize that I've never seen Mom and Dad do anything like that. Even the idea of Dad naked creeps me out.

Becca sits back. "Wow."

There is a silence. I stare at my eggs, which are getting cold.

"You think they're still…?" She trails off.

I've been wondering this myself. "I don't know. Mom didn't seem like she minded leaving Georgetown," I say. Then again, she didn't seem upset about coming back here either. "She and Dad went over to *Freebird* to watch a movie the other night," I tell her. "How weird is that?"

"Very." She blows out a long breath. "What are you going to do?"

I shrug. "Nothing, I guess. I mean, what is there to do?"

"You could talk to your mom."

"Not a chance." I don't know why exactly, but I've never even considered telling Mom that I saw her.

"So…you're just going to go on pretending you don't know?"

"Yup."

"Wow. That's some serious secret." Becca takes a forkful of eggs. "What about Tim? How's he doing with this?"

I feel a flicker of discomfort. "We haven't talked about it."

She stops and stares at me, fork and eggs hovering in midair. "You're kidding."

"What's the point in talking about it?" I say.

"I can't believe this. You both saw it, and you haven't talked about it at all?"

"There's nothing to say," I tell her. Then I take a mouthful of eggs and force myself to eat them like nothing is wrong and there isn't a huge hard lump in my throat.

Becca doesn't say anything for a minute, and I think maybe we're done talking about this. Then she says, "Rachel…look, I feel a bit worried about you guys. You and Tim. He always looks kind of nervous and jumpy, and you're…well, obviously you're not exactly happy."

"I'm fine. We're both fine."

"Yeah. Well, you know if you want to talk about it, I'm always happy to listen."

"Talking won't change a thing," I say.

We spend the whole morning snorkeling. I love snorkeling—it's like being in a whole other world, a peaceful blue world that most people don't even know about. I listen to my breathing through the snorkel, steady and even, and I feel calmer. The water is so clear and it's the same temperature as my body. I could swim all day without getting cold.

Below us, a school of small yellow-and-black-striped fish swarms around: Sergeant Majors. People feed them sometimes, and they flock toward us expectantly. A larger needlefish breezes through their midst, and they scatter. The slight current carries us slowly over a huge coral head, multi-colored and covered with living creatures— spiny black sea urchins, purple fan coral, red Christmas tree worms. A parrotfish glides by, its iridescent greens and purples looking like they've been painted on with a fine brush.

Becca taps me on the shoulder and points silently. A big barracuda, maybe four feet long with gray scarred skin, is swimming right behind us. His mouth is slightly open, showing rows of razor-sharp teeth, and he's watching us the same way we're watching the smaller fish down below. Like we're just as insignificant. It reminds me of what Col said about the stars.

Everything reminds me of Col.

Eventually we get hungry and go back to Becca's boat for lunch.

"So, did you make plans to see Col again?" she asks. She's slicing tomatoes onto a plastic plate.

I frown. "Not exactly. Could I call him?"

"Sure."

I try a couple of times, but he doesn't answer.

"He might be in town," Becca says. "Or maybe he doesn't have his radio turned on."

"We could go into town," I say.

She laughs. "You hoping you'll run into him?"

I try to sound casual, though I know I'm not fooling her. "I wouldn't mind."

"Fine by me," she says. "I have mail to pick up anyway."

"The rudder could be fixed any day now. I don't know how much longer we'll be here," I say. I can't imagine leaving here without seeing Col again. "If we don't run into him, I'll have to find a way to see him tonight."

Becca raises her eyebrows. She puts the knife down and passes me the plate of tomato slices. "How would you swing that?"

"Maybe my parents would let me go out if I said I was meeting you."

"I'm not going to lie to your folks," she warns me. "So don't put me in that position."

I shrug. "Fine then. I'll wait until they're asleep."

Becca picks up a block of cheese and starts to unwrap it. She doesn't say anything for a minute. When she speaks, she sounds uncomfortable. "It's just that I kind of feel like a big sister or something," she says. "Like I'm responsible if anything bad happens. I can't help it. I'm sorry. I know the age difference between us isn't really that big."

"It's okay," I say. "I mean, I wish you would cover for me, but I get it. It's kind of nice." I look away, embarrassed. "I wouldn't mind having you as a big sister."

But I already have a big sister, and she's not here. And if she was, I couldn't talk to her anyway. I usually try not to think about Emma's accident, but now I find myself wondering what it would be like if it had never happened. I wonder what kind of big sister Emma would have been. I wonder what kind of family we would have been.

We were on holiday in Florida when it happened. Mom was six months pregnant with Tim, Emma was six and I was four. So I don't really remember it at all, although

Tim says he does. Which is a typical freaky Tim thing to say, of course. He says that he somehow absorbed Mom's memories *in utero* and that he remembers Mom crying all the time. He says he remembers that he came home from the hospital before Emma did.

Anyway, everything I know—discounting Tim's fantasies—is based on what Mom and Dad told me.

This is what happened: We had spent the morning at the swimming pool at our hotel, which was near the beach. It was the first morning of our holiday, and so there are photographs of those last hours before everything got wrecked. We look happy: Mom big-bellied in a flowered maternity swimsuit with a ruffled skirt, Dad with a beard, Emma with long blond hair held back with barrettes, me half-naked in swim shorts, clutching my one-armed doll.

The hotel was by the beach, but not right on it. It was on the other side of a busy street lined with tourist shops selling ice cream, beach toys and sunblock. Mom and Dad decided to take me and Emma to a restaurant on the beach, figuring we could dig in the sand when we were done eating. So we were all crossing the street together with me holding Mom's hand and Emma holding Dad's. We had made it across safely and were stepping onto the sidewalk when, for some reason, I started to cry, and Mom picked me up. All of a sudden Emma pulled free of Dad's hand and stepped back into the road.

The driver of the car didn't even have time to brake. Emma stepped right in front of him. She was thrown through the air and landed headfirst on the road.

Dad says it was his fault—that if he'd been holding her hand more tightly, it wouldn't have happened. Once, when he'd had a few beers, he told me he could still remember the feeling of her hand slipping out of his.

There's one more thing—something I've never told anyone, something I try not to let myself think about. Last summer when I was making the photo collage for Emma's new room, I looked at all the photographs from that trip. I mean, I really looked at them. And this is what I think: I think I dropped my doll, and Emma turned back to get it. Because that one-armed doll is in my arms in every single photograph up to that point. And after the accident, she never appears again.

Nineteen

We hang around town until dinnertime, but we don't see Col. I head back to the boat in the dark, feeling tired, frustrated and aimless. It's January. Soon we'll leave here—leave behind Will and Col and Becca—and it'll just be our family again, crammed together on this boat for months and months. Sailing to the Turks and Caicos, maybe, and then turning around and sailing back through the Bahamas, and up the coast. Retracing our steps. Every single mile.

Now that I've met Col, I can't stand the thought. I have this sudden crazy idea that maybe he'd take me with him. I imagine the two of us on *Flyer*, standing on the foredeck hand in hand as we sail into the wind, or anchored on a calm night and snuggled together below in the V-berth.

It's a stupid fantasy. It's not going to happen. I know that.

I climb up the ladder and find Tim sitting in the cabin alone. He's holding his rollerblades, and he looks like he's been crying again.

"What's wrong?" I ask.

He doesn't even look up. He just points at the roller-blades. "Look. Look at this."

"Yeah. Your rollerblades. So?"

"You didn't look properly." He clutches them closer. "You didn't even bother looking."

He's sounds like he's about to lose it, so I lean closer and stare at the rollerblades. "Oh…"

The metal buckles are covered with rust.

Tim tries to turn the wheels but they barely move. "I saved up for months to buy these," he says. "Months. And I've hardly even used them on this stupid trip because there haven't even been any proper roads."

"Oh, Tim. I bet you can get new ones when we get back."

Tim glares at me and drops the rollerblades on the floor. "You don't understand anything." He stands up as if he wants to stomp off, but as usual there is nowhere to go.

I remember Becca asking how Tim was doing and feel a pang of guilt and regret and worry. I'm a lousy big sister. I clear my throat and reach out to touch his arm. "Are you okay?"

"Of course I'm not fucking okay," he says.

I don't think I've heard him swear before. "Look," I say. "If you need to talk about what happened, you know, what we saw—Mom and Will…"

He looks at me suspiciously. "Why?"

I shrug. "I don't know." Then I confess. "I told Becca, okay? I mean, I had to tell someone. And then I felt kind of bad that I told you not to talk about it."

"I don't care," he says. "I don't want to talk about it anyway."

I stand there for a moment, scratching one ankle with the inside of my other foot and wondering what to say.

Finally, Tim looks up. "Everything really sucks, doesn't it?"

"Pretty much, yeah." I pick up one of his rollerblades and scratch at the rust with my thumb nail. "I bet Mom would buy you new ones when we get back to the States."

"It doesn't matter. I can't do it anyway." He stares at the floor, back rounded and shoulders slumped. "I thought this trip would change things, but it hasn't at all."

"Change things how?" I expect him to say something about our family, like that maybe Mom and Dad would get along better, but he doesn't.

"I thought maybe I'd learn how to rollerblade like the other kids," he says. "You know. Before middle school."

A picture of a different Tim flashes into my head: tanned and confident, gliding on his blades up to the front doors of the school, maybe waving casually to some girl. I wonder if he thought that this trip would change him. I've always thought he didn't care about fitting in, but maybe I've been wrong.

"You're okay," I say awkwardly. "It doesn't matter that much if you can't rollerblade."

"I know that," he says. "In twenty years, all the dumb-ass jocks who give me a hard time will still be making minimum wage, and I'll be a famous historian." Tim's mouth tightens. "But I have to get through school first."

I plop down beside him on the berth. "Yeah. And we have to get through the rest of the trip before that."

He looks at me. "How come you hate it so much? Other than, you know, what we saw."

I try to be fair. "I don't hate everything about it. I like sailing, when it's not too rough, and I'm not seasick. And I like the islands and how beautiful the water is. I like snorkeling." I think about Becca and Col and Terry. "And I like some of the people."

"So?"

"So…what I can't stand is the way we have absolutely no freedom. No control over where we go or when. It's all on Dad's schedule. Time for schoolwork, time to make dinner, time to clean the cockpit, time to go. He doesn't even consult Mom, let alone us."

"Yeah," Tim agrees. "All the rules. Kind of like being in school twenty-four seven."

"And no privacy," I add, on a roll. "None at all."

He looks at me. "I'm sick of it too."

I wouldn't usually tell him this kind of thing, not back home anyway, but there aren't a lot of other people around to talk to. "I met this guy," I say.

"What guy?"

"Col. He's got his own boat. *Flyer*. It's over in Kidd Cove." I like saying his name, like the feel of the words in my mouth. Col. *Flyer*. Col.

"His own boat? Is he that pilot guy you mentioned before? How old is he?"

"Twenty-five," I say. "Don't tell Mom."

"As if. Anyway, I don't think age is a big deal. My best friend here is Mango, and he's pretty ancient."

"Yeah. And Dad thinks he must be a perv to hang out with a twelve-year-old."

Tim snorts. "Right."

"I know. It's stupid. But they'd freak if they knew about Col."

"We're leaving tomorrow anyway," he says. "The rudder got finished this afternoon, and we're going back in the water in the morning. Mom and Dad are out picking up bread and stuff."

A coldness grips my chest and settles in my belly. "No," I say, "not tomorrow. That's too soon."

He looks at me, forehead wrinkling in surprise. "At least Mom will be away from Will."

"I don't care." I make a face. "Okay, I do. But I don't want to leave Col."

He shrugs. "There's no room for a democracy on a sail-boat, remember?"

"I can't leave without saying good-bye."

"How are you going to do that?"

I glance at my watch. "Shh. I'm going to call Col before Mom and Dad get back." I pick up the radio and this time, Col answers. We switch to a free channel.

"I'm glad you called," he says.

"We're leaving tomorrow. I wanted to say good-bye."

There's a short pause. "That sucks."

I want him to say something more—to say he has to see me tonight—but he doesn't.

"So…what are you up to tonight?" I ask, trying to sound like it doesn't really matter.

"No plans. Want to hang out?"

"Sure," I say. "Can you meet me in town later?"

"Seven at the Two Turtles?"

I hesitate. I'd been thinking I could sneak out again, after Mom and Dad are in bed, but I can't really ask him to meet me at ten thirty. *Go for it,* I hear Jen whispering in my head.

"Okay," I say. "See you then."

Tim looks at me. "How exactly are you going to do that?" he asks. "Mom and Dad won't let you go."

My heart is beating fast and I feel a strange exhilaration. "Then I better leave now," I say. "Before they get back."

"They'll flip out."

I shrug. "Tell them I decided to stay another night at Becca's."

Tim hesitates.

"Come on, Tim." I think about Mom kissing Will. "It's not like they're telling us the truth."

He shrugs. "Okay. But you know they'll kill you when you get back."

"What can they do? Ground me?" I laugh, feeling a little light-headed. "Not let me go to the mall? Or see my friends? Take away my telephone and TV privileges? Oh, wait—they already did all that."

Tim giggles nervously. "Good point." He checks the time. "You better go then. They'll be back any minute."

"I'm going," I say. I pull on a pair of jeans, grab my favorite black hoodie and shove lip gloss and a few bucks in my pocket.

Then I wink at Tim and climb back down the ladder, looking over my shoulder for my parents the whole time.

Twenty

I kill time until seven, and then I walk over to the Two Turtles Inn. To my relief, Col is already sitting at a little table on the patio, wearing faded jeans and a white T-shirt that says *Sail Fast, Live Slow* across the chest. He's drinking a Kalik, and he hasn't seen me yet, so I slow down and stare a little. God, he's gorgeous. I wish Jen could see him.

I cross the patio and sit down across from him. "Hey."

"Hey." He grins, an easy grin that spreads slowly across his face and warms me inside. He hasn't shaved for a couple of days, and it makes him look totally sexy. "I wasn't sure what you'd want so I didn't order for you."

"Kalik's fine," I say.

Col catches the waiter's eye, points to his beer and holds up one finger. "So you really have to go tomorrow?"

"Yeah. It looks that way."

"Man. We're just getting to know each other."

"I know. It sucks."

He shrugs. "That's cruising for you. Meet cool people and say good-bye." He drinks some beer. "Where are you going anyway?"

"Turks and Caicos." A hopeful thought hits me. "Are you going there too?"

Col shakes his head. "No, probably not. Anyway, I kind of like it here."

"Oh." I bite my bottom lip. "Well, I guess it's good-bye then."

"We've still got tonight," he says, winking at me.

I remember what Becca said about him being a player: *Lots of girls. Lots.* I take a long drink of my beer to avoid looking at him for a moment. My cheeks are hot. I don't want to be just another girl.

We stay for a second drink. Col tells me about his brothers and about flying and how he'd wanted to be a pilot even when he was a kid. He talks about his life back home, which makes me feel sad because I'll never be a part of it. Then he stops abruptly and laughs. "You know, they say you should avoid people who sail single-handed. All that time alone makes us a bit crazy. When someone actually listens, you can't shut us up."

I smile at him. "That's okay. I don't mind."

"You're sweet. But come on, tell me more about yourself."

But I can't tell him about my friends, or about school, without letting on that I'm only sixteen. I don't have a job to talk about. I don't even have a dream. What have I always wanted to do? I can't think of anything. I've always wanted to move out, I guess.

So I end up telling him about Emma. I tell him about the accident, though not about my one-armed doll. I tell him about the bleeding in her brain and how the doctors didn't know if she'd ever regain consciousness. I tell him a little about living with her, and how hard it was sometimes, and about how she moved out last year. I tell him about how I visited her every Tuesday, right up until this trip.

He nods. "I had a cousin who lived in a group home. Some of those residents were a lot smarter than people gave them credit for."

"Emma's like that," I say, surprised. "I mean, she obviously couldn't manage on her own. But sometimes when you think she's not really understanding a conversation, she'll come right out with something really surprising. She's perceptive, in her own way. But people don't see that. They only see this skinny girl who walks funny and can't talk quite right. Whenever we go out as a family, people are always staring and saying things."

"People don't think," Col says. "People say things without thinking, all the time. They don't think about the impact their words have."

"And they do things without thinking," I add, picturing Mom and Will. Though of course, I don't know that she wasn't thinking. For all I know, she'd been planning to have an affair. But I doubt it.

"That too," Col says. Then he grins. He pulls some money out of his pocket, lays it on the table and places his empty beer bottle on top. "But sometimes people think too much. Come on. Let's go have some fun."

We walk down to the beach in the dark. It's a clear night with a million stars, and all I want is to sit on the beach with Col and count every single one of them. Every so often I'll think about my parents, and a wave of dread threatens to spoil my mood. Tim's right. They'll kill me when I get back. Or at least Mom will look all sad and hurt, and Dad will give me a long lecture about how disappointed they are and how they just can't understand me, and how a family is like a chain and can only be as strong as the weakest link.

That's me, I guess. I'm the weakest fucking link. Go figure.

I trip over nothing at all and sprawl in the road clutching my ankle. "Shit. Shit. Ow."

Col helps me up. "Last time I walked with you, you were falling over too. Is this a habit of yours?" He looks at my face and his eyes narrow with concern. "Are you okay?"

"I will be," I moan, rocking back and forth in the dirt. "Ow. I'm such a klutz."

"Don't say that," Col says. He reaches down to help me up. "I prefer to think that I keep sweeping you off your feet."

I can't help laughing, even though my ankle really does

hurt. I take his hand, scramble awkwardly to my feet and wince as I try to hobble a few steps.

"Here," Col says. "I'll give you a piggyback." He bends low so I can put my arms around his neck; then he straightens up. "Jeez, you're such a tiny little thing. You don't weigh anything."

My hands are on his shoulders, and I can smell his shampoo. "Yeah, I know. I'm like five-foot-nothing. I got called Shrimp for my entire childhood."

He laughs. "I got called Birdie."

"Birdie?"

"Yeah. Grade one I used to bring toy planes to school all the time, and I never lived it down. At first I got called Pilot, which I liked quite a bit when I was six, but it went downhill from there. Pilot, to Flyer, to Flapper, to Birdie."

"Ouch."

"Yeah. Speaking of which, how's the ankle doing?"

"Mmm. It hurts." Actually it feels a little better, but I don't want him to put me down quite yet.

"Maybe we should go back to my boat instead of going to the beach. Put a tensor bandage on it."

I hesitate. I'd like to go to his boat again. Plus then I could stop worrying that we might run into my parents. But I'm not sure what might happen. I'm not sure what would have happened last night if the rain hadn't started.

"It's up to you," he says quickly. "Whatever you want."

I don't know what he's expecting from me, and that scares me a little. What scares me more is that I almost don't care. "Okay," I say. "Sure. Let's go to your boat."

The cold front hasn't arrived yet, and the dinghy ride out to Col's boat is short and calm. Col helps me out of the dinghy, and I hobble down the steps into the warm and cozy cabin. I sit down and cross my injured ankle across my knee to examine it. A cat jumps up beside me, and I remember the green eyes I saw on the cabin roof when I came here with Becca.

"Hey, you do have a cat," I say. "I thought I saw one last time, but then it disappeared."

"She usually hides when I have company," Col says, stroking her. The cat purrs loudly. "Her name is Orion."

"Isn't Orion a boy?"

He shrugs. "Yeah. But I thought it suited her." He sits down beside me and touches my sandal. "Can I look?"

I unbuckle the strap and slip the sandal off. My ankle looks fine to me.

Col holds my foot gently in one hand and runs the other over my ankle.

I shiver.

"It doesn't look swollen," he says. He flexes it slightly. "Does this hurt?"

"Mmm. Yeah, a little." I don't want him to stop touching me.

"I'm going to raid the first-aid kit," he says. "Back in a flash."

I flick through his CDs. Other than the Jack Johnson he was playing the other night, it's mostly not my kind of music. There's a ton of Caribbean stuff I've never heard of, some other names I don't recognize and some oldies my mom listens to: Neil Young, Joni Mitchell, Simon and Garfunkel.

"Good idea," Col says when he comes back. "Any preference?"

I shake my head. "Just not the Simon and Garfunkel."

He laughs. "Jazz okay?"

"Great," I say, although I'm not really sure what jazz is except for Louis Armstrong, and I couldn't tell you a single song he did.

The music is perfect though—a woman's voice, low and soft and kind of simmering. Over the VHF, I hear the interruption of one boat hailing another. *Tara, Tara. This is Present Moment. Go to channel seventy-two.* Just part of the soundtrack of living aboard. It's considered good etiquette to leave the radio turned on in case another boat needs help.

Col sits down beside me. "Okay, let me get this bandage on for you."

I put my foot on the berth between us. Col lifts it carefully and places it on his thigh. His jeans are ripped across the knee and I can see his bare skin, golden brown against the faded denim. He wraps the tensor bandage snugly around my foot and ankle and then fastens it with a clip.

He looks up at me. "Too tight?"

"No, it feels good." I meet his eyes and look away again. "I wish we weren't going tomorrow."

"I wish you weren't too."

Let me stay with you, I think. Ask me to stay.

Col leans toward me, and we stare at each other for a moment, faces inches apart. Then we start kissing, and I never want to stop.

At some point, Col suggests we move up to the V-berth, where there's a bit more room. Part of me is freaking out—I mean, it's his bed, and I've never been in a guy's bed before. But part of me doesn't care. As long as I'm here, with Col, all that other stuff—Mom and Will, Dad, Emma, Tim—all fades away. All that matters is us: our mouths and our hands and the gentle rocking of the boat and the music spilling out across the water.

So I go with him, and we lie down together on the soft gray and blue blankets. I feel shy and don't know if I should say anything. Col lights a joint and takes a long drag, then hands it to me, laughing and coughing.

"Thanks," I say. The smoke feels hot and scratchy, but I follow Col's lead and hold it in my lungs for as long as I can. Maybe it's stronger this time, or maybe I'm finally doing it right, but within a few minutes I'm definitely feeling something.

"This is..." I can't think of the word. "Nice," I say finally.

Col starts to laugh. He kisses me. "You're nice," he says.

I kiss him back. "You're nice. We're nice." I start to laugh. "This is nice."

"You're really high, aren't you?" he asks, still laughing.

"Umm. I think so."

"Is this still okay?" he asks. His hands are sliding under my shirt, up over my stomach, fumbling with the clasp of my bra.

"Better than okay," I say. "I wish I could stay here with you instead of going with my stupid family."

He looks startled and pauses for a moment, his hands still. I can feel my heart beating hard, and I wish I hadn't spoken. Then he shrugs. "I guess you could, if you're serious," he says lightly. "You could always fly to the States after they cross back over. Meet them in Florida in April."

I stare at him. "Really? I could?" But even stoned, I know that there is no way my parents would let me do this. Not my parents. Not in a million years. I feel a wave of self-pity and then of fury. It's too much, all of it: being dragged away from home and from my friends, Mom and Dad being so awful to each other, Mom screwing around, and now this too—being taken away from Col. It's too fucking much. "You know, my mother is screwing around with that guy, Will," I say.

"Will? Not Will from *Freebird*? The guy who does the cruiser's net?"

"Yeah."

Col laughs. "You're serious? Shit. Does your dad know?"

I shake my head. "Nope. No one knows. I just saw them together one day." Maybe my mom would let me go with Col if I threatened to tell Dad about Will. The thought is immediately followed by a hot wave of shame. I could never do it. I'd hate myself forever.

"Wow. That's pretty intense." He laughs again. "Jesus."

"Yeah." I wish I hadn't brought it up. I don't know why I did. I put my arms around Col's neck and draw him toward me.

He pulls away for a moment, and I feel a flare of anxiety. But then he just lifts his shirt off over his head. I can't stop staring at him. He's so beautiful. An inky constellation is tattooed on his shoulder, and a line of silky dark hair drops from below his belly button and disappears down into his jeans.

I blush and look away.

"Way too many clothes around here," he says.

Within a few minutes, my shirt and bra have joined his shirt in a jumble on the cabin floor. He's lying on top of me, pressing against me, the bare skin of his chest warm against mine. My heart is beating so fast I'm sure he can feel it. "You'd really let me stay with you?" I whisper.

He grins. "Why not?"

Then Dad's voice crackles across the cabin, and my heart crashes to a stop.

Twenty-One

I guess I kind of freeze because Col pushes himself off me.

"What is it? What's wrong?"

"Shh. That's my Dad."

"*Sister Ocean, Sister Ocean*," he says again. "This is *Shared Dreams*."

I hold my breath and pray to anyone who might be listening that Becca is out, or has her radio turned off. I know she won't cover for me.

"That's your Dad?" Col asks. "You want to talk to him?"

I shake my head wildly. "No! He thinks I'm with Becca."

"*Sister Ocean*," Dad calls again. "Please come in. This is *Shared Dreams*."

For once, for perhaps the first time in my life, my prayers are answered. There is no answer. I wait for a minute or two, listening, only half breathing. But all I hear is the sound of soft jazz and water lapping against the hull.

"Shit," Col says.

I start to breathe again. "Yeah. But it's okay. He doesn't know you exist, and Becca could be out all night. If Dad can't get in touch with her, there's nothing he can do. He'll just have to wait until tomorrow to kill me."

He runs his hand slowly down my side and rests it low on my stomach, his fingertips sliding under the waistband of my jeans and grazing the elastic of my underpants. "Tomorrow, huh? Does that mean you're going to spend the night?"

I shiver. I can't believe I'm doing this. I feel like someone else altogether. There's a knot tightening in my stomach, and part of me is scared that I'm making a big mistake. I remember what Becca said: *The first time should be with someone special. Someone you really care about.* But Col is special, I remind myself. And besides, staying the night doesn't necessarily mean I'm agreeing to have sex. Or maybe it does. I don't know.

I nod slowly and keep my eyes on his. "Yeah. I'll stay."

"Good," he says. Then he starts kissing me again, and I try to push Dad's voice out of my head. All I want is to get back to that place where all that matters is right here and right now, but all these other thoughts keep drifting in: What are my parents going to say when I show up tomorrow? What if Col expects me to go all the way? What if I do, and then I never see him again? I remember Becca saying he's been with lots of girls and I wonder how careful he's been. What if I catch some disease or get pregnant?

I wish I could talk to Jen. I didn't even mention Col when I e-mailed her, and I don't know why not. Maybe because home is so far away I can't even imagine it anymore. Or maybe because even Jen would think that twenty-five is too old.

I close my eyes, run my hand through Col's hair and concentrate on the feeling of his lips and tongue meeting mine. I wonder how many other girls he's brought back here. But surely, even if there have been others, this is different.

Col unbuttons my jeans and starts to slide them down over my hips, and I panic and half sit up. "No, I don't know. I don't think…"

He pushes me back down, gently but insistently. "Relax. I'm not going to do anything you don't want me to do."

But I don't know what I want, and for the first time it occurs to me that I'm really alone here with him. What if I want to stop and he doesn't?

"Col…I'm not, you know. I'm not on the pill or anything."

What I mean is *no. We can't do this. I'm not ready.* But that isn't what Col hears. He grins, lifts himself off me and kneels there for a moment. "No problem." He flips open a door in a long shelf that runs along the side of the V-berth and pulls out a box of condoms.

Lots of girls. Lots. I push the thought aside and reach out to him. My hand is shaking. "Not yet."

He smiles. "We've got all night."

It's only a few minutes later when Dad's voice interrupts us again. But this time, he's not hailing *Sister Ocean*.

"*Flyer, Flyer,*" Dad says. "This is *Shared Dreams*."

Col rolls away from me. "Should I answer?"

I shake my head, trying to make sense of this. "Tim must have told him," I say. "The little creep. I can't believe he'd do that."

He looks annoyed. "I should've turned the damn radio off."

"Do it," I say. "Turn it off."

Col stands up and at the same moment, Dad calls again. This time, he calls me by name.

"Rachel, damn it." His voice cracks. "If you can hear this, please answer. It's an emergency. It's Tim."

My first thought is that there's been an accident. That Tim's been hit by a car or drowned. I jump down from the V-berth and almost fall when my injured ankle gives out under my full weight. Col steps past me, grabs the microphone and hands it to me.

"Dad? It's me."

"Rachel. Goddamn it. Get your ass back here, right now."

Dad never talks to me like that. He never swears. And what scares me even more is that he never, never, never disregards radio etiquette by conversing on channel 16.

I start to cry, right there, sitting half-naked on the floor. "Dad? Is Tim okay?" I clutch the microphone and wait for him to reassure me, to say that he's hurt, but he'll be fine. He'll recover.

Instead there's a long pause, and then he says, "He's gone. We don't know where he is."

Not an accident. I feel a flash of relief, followed by a flood of cold anger. Dad scared the hell out of me. He tricked me into answering. "Switch to seventy-two," I tell him. I don't want everyone in Georgetown listening in.

"Just come home. Now."

I ignore him. "Switching to seventy-two." There. He can follow or not. I don't care.

But he does. "Rachel?"

"Tim's probably fine," I say. "He's probably gone for a walk. Maybe he just needed a bit of space."

"It's midnight. Jesus Christ, Rachel. He's not fine. Your mother and I get home and find a note saying he's running away. And then you don't come home either. We've been beside ourselves."

I don't think I've ever heard him so angry.

"I finally tracked your friend Becca down—at the bar, of course—and she said you might be on a boat called—"

"Where's Mom? Can I talk to her?"

"Your mother is still out looking for Tim. God only knows—"

Neither of us are saying *over* and we keep pressing Transmit to talk, cutting each other off, missing the ends of each other's sentences.

"By herself?"

"No, Will's gone with her. From *Freebird*, you know—"

Oh, I know all right. I drop the mike and walk back to the V-berth.

"Ignore him," I say to Col. I climb back up on the bed and reach out to him.

I should have turned the radio off. Dad's still shouting, his voice all crackling with static. "I don't know what the hell you're doing, but I want you back here, right now, or I'm calling the cops."

"He won't," I say. "Besides, we're not doing anything illegal." I put my hands on his chest and smile at him.

Without a word, Col pushes me away.

"Its okay," I tell him. "Dad's all talk." I move closer and slide my hands down lower, across his stomach.

"Damn it, Rachel. Stop." He pushes me away again, more forcefully this time. The radio has fallen silent. "You'd better go."

I start to cry.

He just hands me my clothes and starts dressing.

Twenty-Two

The cold front has arrived at last, blowing up choppy waves in Kidd Cove. Col's wooden dinghy pounds into them. Salt water splashes high and blows back on to us. I wrap my arms around myself and shiver.

I don't say anything. There's nothing to say.

I shine the flashlight toward where the shore must be. It's so dark. Finally we reach the dinghy dock, and Col ties the boat up while I scramble ashore.

"Rachel." He climbs out of the dinghy and grabs my arm. "I guess I'd better walk you back, huh?"

"Don't," I say. "Dad'll freak on you."

"Yeah. I'd rather avoid that if it's all the same to you." He lets me go and steps away without even giving me a hug. It's like I've just become this…liability. He wants to get rid of me with as little hassle as possible. "I guess I'll see you around then," he says.

"Whatever." I take a couple of hobbling steps and start to cry.

"Oh, Jesus. You can't even walk."

I start crying harder. I hate myself for crying, but I can't seem to stop.

Col swears under his breath. He looks back at his dinghy; then he sighs. "Come on then. Let's get this over with."

We're just approaching the unlit boatyard when it occurs to me that I don't necessarily have to go back to the boat. There is nothing I want less than to see either of my parents. Maybe I should go into town and find Becca instead. Or go look for Tim myself. I'm already in so much trouble, it hardly seems to matter.

Col has his arm around my waist, supporting me, and I'm half walking, half hopping. I try putting my weight on my ankle again, and a hot pain shoots up my leg. I swear under my breath. There's no way I can walk into town by myself.

"That your father?" Col asks.

I look up. Dad is pacing back and forth near our boat. Waiting for me.

A second later, he sees us. He spins around and half walks, half runs toward us. Col lets go of me and steps away.

"Rachel." The lights on *Shared Dreams* are behind him, so that his expression is hard to see, but I can hear the anger in his voice clearly enough. "What the hell were you thinking?"

I shrug. "It's no big deal. I was just out with friends." Well, one friend anyway.

As if he's reading my mind, Dad turns to Col. "I don't know who you are or what the hell you think you're doing with a sixteen-year-old, but you can go back to whatever rock you crawled out from under, and stay away from her."

Col doesn't say anything, but I can feel him tensing up beside me. I wonder how angry he is that I lied about my age. He takes a step backward.

"Go on," Dad says. His fists are clenched. I've never seen him like this before and it's freaking me out a little. For a second, I wonder if he might actually hit Col. "Get out of here."

Col looks at me. His face is tight, and I can't tell what he's thinking. Then he just turns and walks away into the darkness.

I watch him go. Tears are welling up in my eyes, and I blink them away, not wanting Dad to see.

"Come on. We'd better catch up with your mother." He shakes his head. "You and Tim, both missing. She was a complete wreck. I hope you're proud of yourself."

"I didn't know Tim was going to take off," I say. "That's not my fault."

He starts walking toward town. "I don't want to hear your excuses."

I take a couple of limping steps and pain shoots up my leg again. "Dad!"

"What?" He turns his head but doesn't stop walking.

"I've hurt my ankle. I can't walk."

"If you think I'm leaving you here by yourself so that you can do whatever you please, you're sadly mistaken." He stops and shakes his head, like I'm just one disappointment after another. "I think you've proven that you can't be left alone. After what you did tonight, I can't trust you. You've broken that trust."

It's something he always says: that trust is something that can be broken. And I'm scared that he's right. Dad wouldn't trust Mom anymore, if he knew about Will. Col won't trust me now that I've lied to him. And I don't think Tim or I really trust anyone.

Can trust be broken so badly that it can't ever be fixed?

I grit my teeth and take another step. Hot tears are squeezing out of my eyes. I watch Dad standing there, staring at me as I hobble forward, and I'm flooded with anger. I'm angry with Dad for being such an ass. I'm angry with him for not knowing that Mom is screwing around on him. How can he be so blind?

"Rachel." His voice is low and controlled, but even so he sounds as angry as I feel. "I don't have the time or patience for your histrionics. So drop the drama and walk. Now."

"I can't!" I'm screaming at him. "You want to go, then go."

And he goes. He doesn't wait for me. He just stalks off toward town. I figure he thinks I'm faking the ankle thing. I hate him. I hate him.

I limp back to the boat, climb up the ladder and sit in the cabin, alone. Dad probably thinks I'm going to call Col. As if. Col probably won't ever speak to me again, now that he knows I lied about my age. My ankle is throbbing. I swing my leg up onto the berth, and a piece of paper falls onto the floor.

Tim's note. His handwriting is horrible, as always, all scrunched up and uneven, wandering up and down as it crosses the page. *I can't take being on the boat anymore,* he's written. *I need to get away for a while. Rachel is at Becca's. Don't worry about me.* Then he's written something else, but it's all crossed out. I squint at it, but I can't read it.

He'd been a mess last night, crying over his rusty rollerblades. What was it he'd said? *I thought this trip would change things, but it hasn't at all.*

For the first time, I feel a sharp pang of fear. What if Tim really isn't okay?

Twenty-Three

I'm lying down, but I can't sleep. My ankle is throbbing, and my thoughts are crashing around, from Tim, to Col, to Dad and Mom and Will.

Everything's coming apart.

It's almost two in the morning when I finally hear someone coming up the ladder. I sit up and listen for Tim's voice.

Instead I hear Will's drawl. "How about Sheila and I stay? We can keep an eye on Rachel while you and Laura keep looking for Tim."

So they haven't found him. Sheila pokes her head down below and shines her flashlight at me.

"She's still here, Mitch."

"Good." That's Dad, sounding relieved that I haven't snuck off again.

"Thank God she's okay." That's Mom. I can tell from her voice she's been crying.

"Hello?" I say. "I can actually hear you, you know."

"Don't be smart," Dad says. He climbs down into

the cabin. "Rachel…Do you have any idea where Tim would have gone? Any idea at all?"

I shrug. "Have you talked to Mango?"

"Mango? No. We didn't see him at the bar."

"But have you checked on his boat?"

They all stare at me like I'm nuts. "You think Tim would go to his boat?"

Duh. "He's his best friend here."

"Goddamn it." Dad is looking at Will. "Maybe you'd better come with me. If Tim's there—"

I can see where this is going. "Mango's a good guy," I say. "If Tim's with him, you don't need to worry. That's the best place he could be, probably."

Mom interrupts me. "I'll go with you, Mitch. Will and Sheila can stay with Rachel."

Great. But at least she's not jumping on the idea that Mango is a pervert.

"Fine," Dad says. He switches on the cabin lights. "And Rachel, you can keep your opinions to yourself. I don't want to get into this now, but you're obviously not the best judge of character."

Jesus. He's one to talk. "I'm sorry," I say for the tenth time. "Okay? I am sorry. If I'd known Tim was going to run away, obviously I wouldn't have taken off."

Dad shakes his head. "That makes it all worse, but I'm not blaming you for that. What I'm upset about is that you promised to come home and you didn't. And you lied to us about where you were—no, worse than that. You left Tim to do the lying for you."

Unbelievable. He actually thinks this is a good time for a lecture. What's the point? It's not like I could feel any worse than I already do. I stare down at my fingernails and suck on my bottom lip.

"Aren't you going to say anything?" Dad asks.

"I already said sorry, okay? What do you want me to say?"

"I want to know what is going on with you. These last couple of weeks you've been completely impossible."

I look up at Dad standing in the cabin, the others all waiting in the cockpit. Maybe I should just tell him the truth. *Jeez, Dad, I've been feeling a bit upset since I saw Mom screwing around with your buddy Will.* Yeah, there's a good option. I suck harder on my lip until it starts to hurt. "I don't know," I say when the silence becomes unbearable.

He shakes his head. "We worry about you, you know. About your safety. I'd like to trust your judgement, but obviously I can't."

"You can," I say sulkily. "There's nothing wrong with my judgement. It's a lot better than some other people's." Like yours or Mom's, for example.

"We'll talk tomorrow," he says coldly.

My heart is beating so hard I feel like it might explode. I want to scream. Punch the walls. Break something. But instead I force myself to lie back down and pretend to sleep as my parents leave and Sheila and Will make themselves at home in the cockpit.

Maybe ten minutes later, I hear someone coming up the ladder and then Sheila's breathless voice. "Tim! Oh my goodness, we've all been so worried."

I jump out of bed and almost fall as my weight lands on my sore ankle. I catch my breath and hobble to the companionway stairs. "Tim?"

He climbs over the rail into the cockpit and looks right at me. "What are *they* doing here?"

I start to laugh. "You're okay?"

"Fine." His face is pale though, and his voice is strained.

"Where have you been?" Will asks sternly. "Your parents have been worried sick."

"Where are they?"

"Taken the dinghy to Mango's boat," I tell him. "I thought you might be there."

He shakes his head. Ignoring Will and Sheila, he climbs down to join me in the cabin.

"Rachel? Tim?" Will starts to follow, sticking his head through the companionway and flashing us a guidance-counselor smile. "Can we come down? We should call your parents; Mitch took the handheld."

"I'll do it," I say. I pick up the mike and hail them. Our dinghy's called *Shared Blessings,* but I just say Mom's name. To hell with radio etiquette. "Mom. It's Rachel."

"Rachel?"

"Tim's home," I say flatly. "He's fine." Then I turn the radio off before she can answer. Sheila has poked her head into the companionway beside Will's, and they're both looking down at me expectantly. I guess they're waiting to be invited in for a cozy little reunion chat. If there is anything that could make this night even worse, it is having Will on the boat with us.

"Thanks for coming," I say, "but Tim and I would really prefer to be alone now."

"Don't be silly," Sheila says. "We were happy to come."

"I'm not being silly," I say flatly.

Her long hair falls forward, half covering her face, and she tucks it back behind her ear. She looks uncomfortable. "I didn't mean it like that," she says. "I just... well, I don't think you two should be on your own."

I think she's the kind of person who enjoys a crisis, the kind who likes to come to the rescue. I wonder if that's why she got stuck with a loser like Will. I feel bad that she's so bewildered by our unfriendliness, but not so bad that I'm going to let her stay. "We don't mind," I say. I look right past her at Will's stupid grinning face. "We want to be left alone."

Sheila turns to Will. "We promised Mitch and Laura we would take care of them."

"Mom and Dad will be back soon," I say. "It's not like we're going anywhere."

Will's not smiling anymore. His face is turning red. "Look, I don't know why you don't want us here but—"

"I think you do know," I say steadily. "I think you know exactly why I don't want you here."

Our eyes lock for a moment, and then Will looks away.

"Come on," he mutters to Sheila. "If they really want to be alone, maybe we should go."

"What did she mean?" I can hear Sheila asking as they climb down the ladder. "What was she talking about?"

Will mutters something about "goddamn teenagers," and then they're gone. Tim and I are alone.

He looks at me, wide-eyed. "Wow."

I giggle, and then despite everything, or maybe because of everything, we both start to laugh uncontrollably.

"It's not funny," I gasp.

"No." Tim looks at me. "I think you do know," he mimics. Then he starts cracking up again.

I think we're actually getting a bit hysterical or something, and maybe I'm still stoned though I don't really feel like I am. I sit back down on the berth. "Jeez, the look on his face…"

"Classic."

Even in the light of the cabin, I can see that Tim's eyes are pink-rimmed and bloodshot. I stop laughing abruptly. "Tim? Why'd you take off tonight?"

"I don't know." He's quiet for a moment. "No good reason, really. You know."

I do know. Only people like Dad believe that everyone always has a reason for the things they do. Like we're these rational, mechanical beings. Like life isn't more random than that.

"Yeah," I say. "Everything has pretty much sucked lately."

Tim sits down beside me on the berth. "I went to look for Mango. I just needed to talk to someone. He's usually pretty good to talk to." He glances at me, his eyes flicking my way for a millisecond. "He listens anyway. He doesn't give lectures or say anything stupid."

I figure we're both thinking about Dad. "So, what happened? You couldn't find him?"

It's so quiet that I can actually hear him swallow.

"I found him," he says. "He was at Eddie's. But he was drunk. He was wandering around with a bottle of rum in his hand, getting in stupid fights. And then he sort of... passed out."

"Ohhh..."

"Yeah. Some of the guys pulled him in the back to sleep it off." He flicks his eyes toward me again. "I guess he actually sleeps back there a lot."

"That sucks."

"Yeah." His eyes flick my way again. "So, I guess we're both in big trouble, huh? You and that guy...are you, you know..."

"None of your business." I stand up and gasp as pain shoots through my ankle again. "Oh, oh. Ow." I glance down at the tensor bandage, and for a moment my stomach tightens. I can almost feel Col's cool hands holding my foot.

Tim follows my gaze. "Hey. What did you do?"

"Just a twist," I say. "Do you think there's any Tylenol around here?"

"First-aid kit," Tim says. "No, actually, wait a sec. Mom has some." He ducks into the V-berth and starts rummaging through her bedside table, then her purse. He pulls out a piece of paper and unfolds it. "It's a letter."

"Are you snooping again?" I ask. "The binoculars thing wasn't bad enough?"

He flushes and starts to put the paper back in her purse. "I wasn't really thinking."

We look at each other for a minute. "Is it to Will?" I ask at last.

He shakes his head. "I don't know. I didn't even read anything yet."

There is a long pause, and then I say, "Okay. Hand it over. I'll read it."

Tim passes me the paper. I open it up and see a whole page of small tidy writing. "It's to Emma," I say, surprised.

He frowns. "That's weird."

It is weird. Mom writes to Emma every week, but usually just short postcards with bright pictures on the front. Not long letters like this. Emma can't read and doesn't have the attention span to listen to more than a few sentences.

"Are you going to read it?" Tim asks.

I already am. "Okay. This doesn't make sense...I mean, Emma wouldn't understand any of this..."

He sits down beside me and reads over my shoulder as I start to read out loud.

"*Dear Emma, Lately I've been thinking that being a mother is all about hearing what isn't said: reading the silences, noticing the absences. If a mother is vigilant enough, maybe she can reach out across the ever-growing gaps before they become too wide. Maybe she can grasp the last threads of childhood and hold on tightly. I forgot to be vigilant once. I let my attention lapse for a second and your life was forever changed. And now I feel like Rachel and Tim are slipping away too. Maybe this trip was a bad idea. Or maybe we just left it too late."*

I stop reading because my voice is starting to shake. I look up at Tim.

"We shouldn't be reading this," he says. His eyes are wide and shocked.

I shove the letter back into Mom's purse. My hand is shaking. "She wasn't really going to send it to Emma, was she?"

He shakes his head. "No, it's like...it's more like a journal or something. Only she writes it like she's talking to Emma."

"Not our Emma."

"No." He hesitates. "Maybe...maybe it's an imaginary Emma. Like, you know, who Emma might have been."

I swallow hard. "Do you really remember the accident? Or was that just something you made up?"

Tim looks uncomfortable. "I don't know. You know when you look at an old picture a lot of times, say of a place you've been? And then after a while you can't tell if you remember the place itself or just the picture?"

I nod.

"Well, it's like that. I have these things that feel like memories, but I don't know if they really are."

Anxiety is buzzing inside me like electricity, a low crackling hum in my bones. I'm wondering whether it's totally stupid to ask Tim if he knows why Emma stepped back into the road, when we hear Mom and Dad coming.

Twenty-Four

"I don't want to have to talk to them," Tim says. "You know. About tonight."

"Me neither." I feel trapped.

"Let's pretend we're asleep."

"As if." But I switch off the light and hop into my bed anyway. Tim ducks into the aft cabin. Our berths are only a few feet apart. We lie there in the darkness, waiting, and I hear Tim start to cry. His breath comes in little gasps.

I've been a lousy big sister to him.

"Tim?" I whisper. "I'm sorry I wouldn't let you talk to me about Mom and Will. About what we saw. You know."

I can hear his crying slowing down, his breathing getting calmer.

"It's okay," he says at last. "I didn't want it to be real either."

I open my eyes, but I can't see his face in the darkness. Mom and Dad are climbing up the ladder, but I ask him anyway. "How did you know that's why I didn't want to talk about it?"

His whisper is so soft I can barely make out his words. "That's what we all do, right? If we don't talk about something, it isn't real."

We hear steps into the cockpit outside.

"Kids?" Mom calls softly. "Are you there?"

They both climb down the ladder. "Where the hell are Will and Sheila?" Dad mutters.

Despite the seriousness of it all, and the knowledge that I'm probably about to be grounded forever, I almost giggle. Seeing that stupid, fake grin wiped off Will's face...

The light switches on and I sit up, blinking.

Mom looks like absolute hell. Her hair's blown all over the place, her thin face is all puffy and her eyes are swollen from crying. She looks about ten years older than she did this morning.

"Mom?" I feel a sickening stab of guilt. I didn't mean to do this.

She gives me a quick hug; then she turns and bends down to hug Tim. His eyes are open, but he's still lying there, all stiff, like he's not sure whether to keep faking sleep.

Dad steps closer to me and for a second, I think he might hug me too—even though he almost never does—but instead he bends closer and sniffs. When he speaks, his voice is practically dripping disgust. "Christ. You've been smoking pot, haven't you."

It's not a question, the way he says it, so I don't answer. I clamp my mouth shut. If I let myself say anything at all, I'm going to tell him to fuck off. And that's probably a bad idea.

"Mitch, how about we leave it for now? They're both exhausted. We're upset…" Mom trails off and puts her hand on his shoulder.

He shrugs it off like it's a fly that's just landed there. "Family meeting," he says. "First thing tomorrow."

I'm woken in the morning by the sound of Will's voice blasting over the VHF. I guess *first thing* means after the cruiser's net. Dad wouldn't let a little family crisis disrupt the morning routine. Not him. No, it's like his life depends on all his rules and schedules. If he let them slip, chaos and randomness would take over.

"Good morning, Georgetown!" Will is saying. He sounds just as phoney and cheery as always, although he can't have had much sleep.

I hope he had none at all. I hope he was up all night wondering how much I knew and whether I'd tell Sheila. She probably has no idea he cheats on her. I sit up slowly. My throat is dry and scratchy, and my mouth tastes sour. I wiggle my foot tentatively. My ankle still hurts, but not like it did last night.

Mom and Dad are already up, sitting side by side in the cockpit. I squint my eyes against the sun and watch them. From this angle, I can see only their legs and the lower part of their bodies. Dad's expanding beer gut. I wonder what it's like for Mom, sitting there with Dad and listening to Will's voice.

I wonder if she's in love with Will.

I stand up, careful not to put too much weight on my bad ankle, and turn off the radio. "Do we have to listen to this?"

"Turn that back on," Dad snaps.

Usually, we all tiptoe around Dad's rules. I wonder what he'd say if he knew he was insisting on listening to the man his wife is having an affair with. It occurs to me that I could just open my mouth and tell him, just like that.

The thought makes me dizzy. "I don't want to listen to it," I say.

Dad sticks his head through the companionway door and stares at me. "I think we've noticed that it all seems to be about what you want lately. I've had about enough of your selfishness, Rachel. I've had it up to here with your attitude."

I don't say anything. My ankle is itching under the tensor bandage. Behind me, I can hear the slippery rustle of Tim getting out of his sleeping bag.

"I don't know what to do with you," Dad says. His face is red. "We've given you every opportunity, and you seem to be intent on throwing it all away."

"Mitch." Mom puts her hand on his shoulder.

He shrugs her hand off, just like he did last night. "The way you're going," he tells me, "you'll go nowhere. You've got choices to make, Rachel." He holds up one finger. "And your life is the sum of your choices."

"Spare me."

"Don't you dare roll your eyes at me."

We stare at each other, neither of us budging an inch. My heart is pounding.

"Mitch." Mom's voice is louder this time. "Just…let them get up, okay? Let's all have breakfast. There's a lot to talk about and there's no point…" She trails off and makes a helpless gesture. "What you two are doing here isn't going to get us anywhere."

"Goddamn it, Laura. Don't undermine me."

I step closer to the stairs and duck a little, so that I can see Mom's face. She's so tall, taller than Dad. She's standing beside him in the cockpit, her hair pulled back into a tight ponytail, a baseball cap shading her eyes. "Listen, Mitch—"

"We agreed to present a united front. Rachel's behavior isn't acceptable, and I'd like you to back me up."

"I just don't think—"

"Jesus Christ, Laura. The way you always make excuses for her doesn't help. In fact, that's probably at least half the problem right there."

She stares at him. It's like they've both forgotten Tim and I are here, listening. "Are you blaming me for what happened last night?"

He doesn't answer her question. "Are you with me or not?"

Mom just looks at him, her face unreadable. She looks like she's thinking about something, like she's a thousand miles away. After a long minute, Dad says, "Laura?"

She shakes her head and I can see tears glinting on her cheeks. "No," she says. "No, Mitch. I'm not." She steps away from him, swings her legs over the stern rail and climbs down the ladder.

Dad leans over the edge of the boat. "Laura! Goddamn it, Laura. Get back here. Let's talk about this."

She doesn't even answer.

I step away from the companionway as quietly as I can and sit back down on my berth. I hope Dad will just forget that Tim and I are down here, though it seems unlikely. Tim is standing behind me, wide-eyed, still in the clothes he was wearing last night. I guess I am too. I glance down at my faded jeans and remember Col's hands unbuttoning them and sliding them down over my hips.

"I'm going with her," Tim says. He pushes past me and scrambles up the steps and out to the cockpit.

"Wait a minute," Dad says. "We need to talk."

"I'm going with Mom," Tim says, and he hops over the railing and down the ladder.

Great. Just me and Dad. For a second, I contemplate running after Tim, but given that I can barely walk, I discard the idea. Besides, I don't want to be with Mom either. I close my eyes for a second and picture Col's face. I wish I could go away with him. But then I remember how he acted after Dad's call on the radio. He couldn't get rid of me fast enough. And then when Dad told him how old I was...

I hope he doesn't hate me.

Dad climbs down into the cabin, a mug in one hand. He dumps a spoonful of instant coffee into his mug, pours hot water from the kettle on top and mixes it carefully. Three stirs one way, three stirs the other way.

"That guy you were with last night..." He doesn't look at me.

"Col."

"Whatever. How old is he?"

"Twenty-five."

Dad shakes his head again. "I should've called the police."

"Dad! Don't be...that's crazy. Anyway, it's not Col's fault. I told him I was eighteen."

He closes his eyes for a second. "Jesus. He'd have to be an idiot to believe it. You look more like fourteen." He opens his eyes and looks right at me. "Please tell me you didn't have sex with him."

My face is on fire. "I didn't. Oh my god, Dad. I can't believe you just asked me that."

"Your mother should be having this conversation with you, not me," Dad says.

Something inside me flashes hot and angry. "I bet you'd like that," I say. "I bet you'd like her to take care of everything so that you could just go back to ignoring us."

He stares at me. "What are you talking about?"

I'm practically screaming now and I'm embarrassed, sort of, to be so out of control, but I can't seem to stop. "I'm talking about how you never pay any attention to anything Tim or I do. I'm talking about the fact that you've been practically living at your office since forever and maybe you haven't even noticed that I'm not a little kid anymore."

"That's not true."

"It is so true. You blame Mom for everything, but at least she tries. You've never even bothered. You have all the time in the world for the stupid screwed-up teenagers you see at work, but no time at all for us."

Dad's voice is low and angry. "You think I want to work all the time? Do you have any idea what it costs to pay for Emma's care? Or to be able to save for university for you and Tim?"

"I bet you couldn't name a single one of my teachers from last year," I say. "I bet you never even looked at my report card. Christ, Dad, you barely even made time to visit Emma."

He turns away from me and slams his palms down flat on the counter. He stands there for a moment, and I can hear him breathing hard. I bet he'd like to slap me and for some reason I almost wish I could make him do it. Make him lose control. After a minute, he turns around and faces me again. His face is very red. "Rachel, get a grip on yourself," he says. "This is...not acceptable."

"What the hell do I have to do to get you to pay attention?" I ask, only slightly more quietly. "Maybe if I started smoking crack? Or developed an eating disorder? You find those interesting, right? What would you prefer?"

"Rachel! Stop it!" His voice cracks and for the first time ever, I think I can see tears in his eyes. Actual tears.

I stare at him and say nothing.

He slowly sits down beside me. "You know I love you and Tim and Emma. I love you all so much. You're the most important things in my life."

"You sure hide it well," I say quietly. I stare at the faded denim of my jeans, pulled tight across my thighs, and feel like I'm crumbling inside. Like I needed every bit of that anger to hold me together, and now that I've let some of it escape I might just fall apart. "I don't know anything anymore," I whisper. "I don't know who Mom is, and I don't know who you are. I don't know why you two stay together. And I don't know why you bothered to bring us on this trip."

Dad sighs. The maybe-tears are gone, and I wonder if I imagined them. "What do you want, Rachel? First you say I should spend more time with you instead of working and then you complain about this trip. The whole point of which was to spend time together."

"The trip was your thing," I say. "It was your dream. You were the only one that really wanted to do this trip. You never asked us what we wanted."

There is a long silence. Finally Dad says, "Okay, Rachel. I'm listening. You now have my full and undivided attention. What is it that you want?"

I don't know what to say. I want everything to be different. I start to cry, stupid hot tears that I don't want him to see. I stand up and walk to the stairs. Outside in the cockpit, Tim is crouched down, watching us. I didn't hear him come back and I wonder how long he's been standing there listening.

"We want you and Mom to stop fighting," he says. His voice is loud and unsteady. "We want everything to be okay again."

Dad sighs again. His hands are laced together so tightly the knuckles are white. "We want that too," he says. "We want that too." Then he turns away and takes his coffee up to the V-berth.

I watch the thin wooden door slide shut behind him. Apparently the conversation is over.

Twenty-Five

I grab a couple of slices of bread and climb outside to join Tim. Dad stays down below, drinking coffee, while Tim and I sit in the cockpit, wondering what to do. It doesn't look like the family meeting is going to happen anytime soon.

"Did you catch up with Mom?" I whisper.

Tim nods. "But she said she needed to be alone for a while. To think."

A cold fear settles into the bottom of my stomach. Everything feels unpredictable. Fragile. I look out at the boatyard. Around us, on cradles, sit a dozen or more boats with varying degrees of damage. Several have hit reefs or rocks and one actually has a huge hole in the side of its hull. A couple look like they've been sitting here for years, slowly rotting. Beyond the boatyard, the blue water of the harbor sparkles in the morning sun. I wonder if Mom has gone to see Will.

"Do you think…," I start to say; then I let my voice trail off. There is no point in talking about any of it. Besides,

I'm sure Dad can hear us. I want to get off the boat, but I know what Dad will say. There's no use asking.

We sit there in silence. I eat my bread. It tastes like nothing at all, but I'm starving. I could cram slice after slice into my mouth. After a while, Tim lies down on the deck and goes to sleep. I try to do the same, but I have this awful feeling of foreboding—that low thrum of anxiety is buzzing around inside me again. I can't sleep.

It's at least an hour before Mom comes back. She sits down in the cockpit beside me. "Did you have the meeting without me?"

"Not exactly."

She sighs. "Sorry I left. Is your father...?"

"Down below."

Mom disappears down below for a minute, and I can hear the two of them whispering. I can't make out the words, but it's obvious they're arguing.

Tim opens his eyes. I think maybe he's only been pretending to sleep. "They're going to get a divorce, aren't they?"

He's asked me that question before. Lots of times. I've always said, "How would I know?" or "Don't be stupid." And I've sometimes thought it'd be better if they would get a divorce and get it over with. Now though, I'm not so sure. I wrap my arms around myself, suddenly feeling chilled. "Maybe," I say. "Maybe."

After a while, they call us to come down below for "a little talk." They're sitting side by side on the port side berth, so I guess they've gone back to the idea of presenting a united front. Tim and I sit down across from them.

I feel like there isn't enough oxygen for us all.

Mom looks nervous. She crosses her legs first one way and then the other; she twists her wedding ring around on her finger. I shoot Tim a sideways glance, but he's watching Mom.

"Well," she says at last, "I want to say first that I'm so glad you two are both home safely. Last night…" Her voice catches, and she swallows so hard I can see the movement in her throat. "If anything had happened to either one of you…"

There's this awful thick silence and I know we're all thinking about Emma.

"I'm sorry," I say.

Tim nods. "Yeah. Me too. I just sort of needed to get away."

Mom sniffs a bit, and Dad clears his throat.

"I guess this need to get away is contagious," Mom says. Her voice catches again, and she starts crying. "Damn it."

There's not enough air down here. There really isn't. My heart is racing. "What do you mean?"

Mom looks at Dad and he gives this little shrug as if to say, *Go ahead. Tell them yourself.*

"I'm going to Nassau for a few days," she said. "Your father and I…we've been having some problems. I need a little space. To think." She reaches a hand out to us, but we both just sit there staring at her. "I'd like you and Tim to come with me."

"What about Dad?"

She glances at him. When he doesn't say anything, she answers for him. "He'll stay here with the boat. Make sure the work gets finished, get the boat back in the water."

"Will we come back?" I'm thinking about Col and whether I'll see him again.

"Of course. I think so. But…" She stops.

But maybe not to stay? Was that what she meant? Or perhaps, But maybe not to your father?

"Like, you mean we'd stay in a hotel or something?" Tim asks.

He's trying to picture it, I think. To make it real. Because right now, none of this feels real at all.

A voice calls out from outside. "Rachel!"

I stand up, climb out to the cockpit and look over the side of the boat. Becca is staring up at me, with the sun low in the sky behind her, and her fuzzy blond dreads are glowing in the morning light.

"Hey."

"Hey. Look, I heard…" She breaks off. "Well. Want to come for a walk?"

I nod. "Just a second." I poke my head back into the cabin. "Becca's here. I'm going to go talk to her."

Dad shakes his head. "I don't think so."

"Oh, let her go, Mitch." Mom stands up. "She needs to talk to someone. Anyway, what difference does it make?"

I don't wait for an answer. I look at Tim, sitting on the berth with his long legs folded up in front of him and his shoulders hunched. I hesitate for a second; then I hold out a hand toward him, beckoning. "Tim, why don't you walk with us? We can check if there are any messages at Exuma Market."

"Rachel…" Dad frowns.

Tim ignores him. "Okay. Sure," he tells me.

The three of us walk into town together. My ankle hurts, a little stab of pain with every step, but at least I can walk. I tell Becca that we might be going to Nassau for a few days, but I don't get into the reasons for it. What I really want to talk about is Col. Not in front of Tim though. I glance sideways at him and half wish I hadn't invited him along.

When we get to Exuma Market, Mango is sitting outside in a patch of shade. He waves to Tim. Tim's face splits with a wide grin. "I'm gonna go talk to Mango."

"Meet you back here in half an hour?" I say. Tim nods.

As soon as he's out of earshot, Becca grabs my arm. "Look, Col called me this morning, right after the net. He told me what happened last night."

"He did?" I wonder how much he said.

"Just that you were over there and then your dad called." She squeezes my arm sympathetically. "What a mess, hey? I'm so sorry."

I feel like the bread has turned to a big lump halfway down my throat. "Yeah. A big mess." I think about Col's lips on mine, and then I remember the look on his face before he walked away. "Dad told him how old I am," I whisper. "Does he hate me?"

She hesitates; then she shakes her head. "Of course he doesn't hate you."

"He's not mad?"

There is a long pause, and I can see Becca choosing her words carefully.

"He was upset. He says your dad looked at him like he was some kind of child molester or something."

I swallow and taste tears at the back of my throat. "He did."

Becca pulls me close and gives me a hug. I hold onto her shoulders and try not to cry. "I just...I didn't think he'd be interested if he knew I was only sixteen."

She nods. "I know. Well, he shouldn't have been."

"I don't think age should matter," I argue, pulling away. "Not if two people really like each other."

Becca is quiet for a minute. "I don't know," she says. "Twenty-five is a lot different than sixteen."

"You don't even like Col," I say. For some reason I feel like picking a fight with her, which is stupid as she is the only friend I have here.

She shrugs. "I think you could do a whole lot better."

"What's that supposed to mean?"

"Seriously? Same thing I said before. He's a player."

I don't say anything.

"I think this all means a lot more to you than it does to him." Becca pulls on her lower lip with her teeth and looks at me as if she's trying to decide whether to say more.

"What is it?"

"Don't answer this if you don't want to, but how far did things go with you guys?"

I look around. Tim and Mango are still sitting in the shade, a couple of cruisers are waiting impatiently for the store to open, a cluster of local kids are kicking a Hacky Sack around. No one is paying any attention to us. No one is close enough to hear. I sit down on the curb, and the concrete is warm on the backs of my thighs. "Far enough," I tell her. "Not, you know. We didn't have sex."

She sits down beside me. "I mean, it's none of my business."

"That's okay." It's a relief to have someone to talk to about it all. "I think we might have though. You know, if Dad hadn't called."

"Well, if you do, be careful. Okay?"

"Yeah." I make a face. "I think Dad figures I'm going to be a pregnant, drug-addicted drop-out by my seventeenth birthday. I got the big lecture about making wise choices blah, blah, blah."

"It's his job to worry," she says. "I know you're pissed off at your folks, but I don't blame them for being concerned."

I hate it when she starts sounding more like a parent than a friend. Like nineteen is so much older than sixteen. Then something else occurs to me. "Wait a minute. You said, be careful. Does that mean you think he still might be interested?"

"Oh, Rachel." She sounds exasperated. "I don't know. He might be. I just don't think he should be."

I feel a little better for a second, and then I crash back down. "I bet I wrecked everything. He's never going to forgive me for lying to him."

Becca shrugs. "I don't know. Honestly, I think he just doesn't want your dad to beat him up."

"But you don't think it's over? You think he'd still talk to me?"

"Maybe. I don't think he's really mad at you or anything. He just doesn't like hassles." She shrugs again. "This is a guy who's probably never worked a day in his life, you know? He's into keeping things simple."

For a second, I let myself remember how Col pushed me away when Dad said he'd call the cops, and how he didn't even say good-bye. My stomach tightens uneasily, and I push those memories aside. Instead I think about our first kisses, up on the windswept foredeck of Becca's boat. I think about him piggybacking me back to his dinghy and telling me how he used to get called Birdie. I think about him bandaging my ankle. I think about how it felt to lie so close together, skin to skin.

I wish I could erase the way the night ended.

But I don't even get a chance to call him. When Tim and I get back to the boat, Mom tells us that she's booked us on a flight to Nassau for this evening. As in, the plane actually takes off six hours from now. Dad's gone off somewhere, probably to drink beer at Two Turtles. Mom's fussing around, packing her stuff and muttering about airport shuttles and hotel bookings. Tim and I throw a few clothes into daypacks, toss in our toothbrushes and then sit there, staring at each other and wondering what to do next.

What I really want to do is to call Col before we leave, but I can't do that in front of Mom and Tim. Not to mention anyone else who might be listening to their VHF. As usual, there is no privacy at all. Besides, even if I was alone with him, I think I'd be too scared of what he might say.

Twenty-Six

The airport shuttle stop is right in front of Exuma Market.

We look down the empty road. The sun is low, the sky a dusky dark blue, huge and cloudless, big as an ocean. No bus anywhere in sight.

Mom has a decent travel bag because she planned to fly home to see Emma a couple of times, but Tim and I have only our daypacks. I wonder how long we'll be gone. Mom is rifling through her purse, looking for something, and I take the opportunity to watch her without her knowing it. She looks gorgeous, as usual. Tall and long legged and effortlessly glamorous. Ever since I saw her with Will, she seems so unfamiliar. Like she's got this whole secret life, and she's not just our mother after all.

Even though it's starting to get dark, she's still wearing her sunglasses. Probably because she's been crying, but you'd never know it.

She looks up and sees me staring at her. I drop my eyes quickly and turn away. I wish Col would come walking down the road. Then I see that someone is walking toward us. For a second, a half second, I hope—but it's not him.

It's Will.

Tim looks at me, and I know what he's thinking. "I'm going in to grab a Coke," he says. "You want anything?"

I shake my head, and I don't budge. "Nope." I don't blame Tim for not wanting to be around Will, but I don't see why Mom should get to be alone with him to say good-bye.

"Be quick," Mom tells Tim. "The shuttle will be here any minute."

Will stops in front of us. "Sheila and I stopped by your boat." He gestures in the general direction. "Sheila made some cookies for the kids. Mitch told me you're going to Nassau." He looks bewildered. "Weren't you even going to say good-bye?"

"It was a last-minute decision," Mom says.

"Yeah, but still."

Mom doesn't say anything.

Will looks at me, and I can actually see him stifle a sigh. A little intake of breath which he lets out slowly and almost silently, lips still pressed together.

I look back at him and smile like I don't have a clue.

Behind them, I can see our bus coming down the road.

"I guess we have to go," I say.

Mom nods. "Yes." She turns to look for Tim.

He's sprinting toward us, Coke can in hand. He stops a few feet away, looks at Mom, then at Will, then back at me. He picks up his bag and steps onto the bus, and Mom and I follow.

The plane ride is so short. Forty minutes. It took us days to travel this distance on *Shared Dreams*. Places seem so much farther apart when you're traveling by boat. It's strange to think that we could just get on another plane and be back in Canada in a few hours.

Mom rents a car at the airport and drives us to a hotel. Occasionally one of us points out something interesting as we drive along, but none of us is talking much. Questions hang in the air, unspoken: Are you going to leave Dad? Is this permanent? Will we all sail home together or is the trip over? Outside the window, the air is hot and heavy, thick with traffic noises. Streetlights and trees flash past; horns honk loudly. I realize I haven't been inside a car for months.

The hotel is pretty basic, but after months of living on a boat it feels like a palace. Tim and I bounce on the beds, flop down and stretch out like starfish, luxuriating in the spaciousness. We wash our faces in hot soapy fresh water and dry them on soft white towels. Mom sits on her bed and writes in a spiral notebook. I wonder if she's writing to Will, or journaling to sort out her thoughts. Or maybe she's writing more weird letters to Emma.

I already know that if she leaves her purse behind, I'm going to look.

We eat hamburgers at the restaurant next to the hotel and go to bed early. Not talking about anything is becoming a strain. I'm still waiting for the lecture about taking off with Col last night, but Mom seems lost in her own thoughts. I don't know why she wanted Tim and me to come to Nassau with her. Still, it beats staying on the boat with Dad, getting one lecture after another.

Despite everything, I sleep well. Being in a real bed, I guess, instead of a foam berth that's not even two feet wide. When I wake up, it's dark, and for a moment I can't think where I am. An obnoxiously loud alarm clock is buzzing—I guess whoever slept here last set it, because I sure didn't. I fumble around and switch it off. The digital clock says it's 8:00 AM. I turn on the light and sit up.

Mom's not in her bed. There's a note on the dresser: She's gone for a run.

Tim walks over to the window and throws open the heavy curtains. Sunlight streams in. "There's a pool. We could swim."

"I didn't bring my swimsuit."

"Me neither." He makes a face. "We could wear our clothes."

I grin. What the hell. It's not like we're ever going to see any of these people again.

While Tim's in the washroom, I check Mom's purse. The spiral notebook isn't in it. I'm desperate to know what's going to happen, but I don't want to ask. I don't want to rush Mom into a decision. If she decides to leave Dad, I don't want it to be my fault.

The water in the pool is warm and blue. It's almost the same color as the water in Red Shanks, but without any subtlety. It's the turquoise blue of the paint on the cement bottom. We stand on our hands, toss a ball back and forth, swim lengths and turn somersaults. Then we lie on white plastic deck chairs while our clothes cling to us and drip onto the hot concrete.

I turn my head to one side to face Tim. His arms are folded behind his head, his eyes are closed and his face is turned to the sun. For the first time, I notice that my geeky little brother is turning into an actual teenager. I mean, a guy, not a kid. He has muscles in his arms and shoulders that weren't there before this trip.

He opens one eye. "Are you staring at me?"

"Yeah."

"Why?" He sits up. "What is it?" He looks down at himself.

I look away from him and squint up into the bottomless blue of the sky. "Nothing. I was just thinking that you look different. Like maybe you've grown or something."

"You think so?" he asks hopefully.

I remember his rollerblades and his worries about starting middle school. "You look good," I say. "If you weren't my little brother, I'd even say you might end up being kind of cute."

He rolls onto his side and looks at me suspiciously. "Really? Are you being serious?"

"Yeah, really." I grin at him. "You know, eventually. Like in ten years maybe."

Tim picks up his wet towel and tosses it at me. "Thanks a lot."

"No problem."

We lie in the sun for a while in a comfortable silence. Finally, Tim says softly, "Rachel?"

"Mmm?"

"I heard what you said to Dad about not knowing why he and Mom stay together."

I roll on to my side to face him. "And?"

"Well…it almost sounded like you'd rather they did split up."

I think about it for a moment, trying to sort out what I feel. "I don't want them to split up," I say at last. "It's just that if they're going to do it, I wish they'd get it over with." I look at him to see if he understands. He's looking straight up at the sky, and I can't tell what he's thinking. "I hate not knowing what's going to happen next," I say.

"But you'll never know that," Tim says.

My mind fumbles backward through this past year: Emma moving out, me finding the photos of my one-armed doll, meeting Jen and drifting away from Mom, my parents fighting all the time, leaving on this trip, Mom kissing Will…you'd think that there would be clues buried somewhere in the past that could tell us something about the future.

Tim sits up and wraps his arms around his knees. "It's weird how Mom hasn't said anything about last night. Me running off, or you being with that guy."

"Col. Yeah." I make a face. "Typical Mom. Denial in action."

He is quiet for a moment. Then he speaks in a low voice, almost a whisper. "Do you think you'll ever ask her? You know. About…"

A week ago, I would've said something cutting or maybe just told him to shut up. I don't know why exactly, but something has changed between us. I look at his green eyes, so much like Mom's. "About what we saw? About Will?" I can't imagine it. "Do you think I should?"

"I don't know."

"If she's leaving Dad anyway, I guess it doesn't really matter."

"Denial in action," Tim says.

I stare at him for a moment. Then I pick up my book and pretend to read.

Twenty-Seven

Mom finally shows up just before noon. She walks along the edge of the pool so that her shadow falls across our loungers. She stops at our feet. "Look at you two. You know, there's a great little swimsuit shop next door. Maybe we should pick up new suits for you both. Your old ones were starting to look pretty ratty anyway."

I squint up at her. Her hair's wet from the shower, and she's smiling. It's like she's pretending we're here on holiday or something.

"How long are we going to stay?" I ask.

Her smile slips. "I know this must be hard for you both. I'm sorry."

I wait.

"I need some time to think," she says. "I guess you both know your father and I haven't been getting along so well."

You'd have had to be deaf and blind to miss it.

She sighs. "Well, I need to make some decisions. And I couldn't think straight on that boat." She pauses and when she speaks again, her voice is hard-edged. "It was... claustrophobic. I couldn't take it anymore."

All of a sudden there is a cold feeling in my belly and the buzzing is back, so strong it makes me want to throw up. I can't stand not knowing, but I don't want to hear this either. I sit up and wrap my towel around myself, not looking at her.

"Last year, we actually talked about taking some time apart." She takes off her sunglasses and folds them up. "We saw a counselor together a few times, and we decided to try to make it work. And to make things better with you and Tim too."

"All those family dinners," I say, glancing up at her.

"Yes, all those family dinners. And this trip too. Obviously that hasn't really worked out." She slips the sunglasses into the pocket of her cargo shorts. "I guess maybe it wasn't realistic to expect it to solve anything."

"You said the trip was about Tim and me," I remind her.

"She did?" Tim sits up. I'd forgotten he was there. "Did you say that, Mom? How come?"

Mom shakes her head. "It was about all of us. The whole family."

It seems to me like she and Dad say whatever is convenient in the moment. "Not the whole family," I point out. "Not Emma."

"Emma is an adult," Mom says. "She'll always be part of the family, but she's grown up and moved out."

"Not really," I say. "Maybe you'd like to think that, but she still needs us."

"Rachel." She tilts her head and studies my face. "We're not abandoning her, but life has to go on. Everything has revolved around her for years. I don't think that's been entirely healthy for you or for Tim."

I think about all the vacations that were cut short because Emma couldn't deal with the change in routine, all the school plays and soccer games that Mom or Dad came to alone because it was impossible to find babysitters for Emma, all the dinners that ended with Mom in tears because Emma would throw food if she got frustrated at being left out of the conversation.

"I love Emma," I say softly.

Mom looks like she might cry. "Oh, honey. We all love Emma. That's why it's been so hard."

"Mom." I dig my nails into my palms. "I was wondering. I was looking at some old photos and...do you remember that doll I used to have? That one-armed doll?"

Her eyes widen. "Yes, you took it everywhere."

"What happened to it?" I hold my breath and listen to the *thud, thud, thud* of my heart against my ribs. It feels like it's trying to escape.

"I didn't know you remembered that doll," she says slowly.

My throat tightens. I glance over at Tim, wondering if he knows, if he really does remember the accident, but he just looks confused and maybe a bit curious.

Mom looks past us, at the row of palm trees that rings the pool area, but she looks like she's seeing something else. "When Emma's accident happened, we all went to the hospital together," she says. "It was an awful place to bring a four-year-old, but we didn't have a choice; we had to bring you." She looks back at me. "Somehow your doll got left behind in the emergency room."

I swallow. "Are you sure? In the emergency room?"

"Oh, I'm sure. One minute you were sitting on a chair, half asleep with that doll in your arms while we were talking to the doctors. Then we carried you up to the intensive care unit where they took Emma after the surgery and when you woke up, you started screaming because the doll was gone." She shakes her head. "You were devastated. You never slept without that doll. We checked the lost and found for days, but it never turned up."

"So it got lost in the hospital," I say. I have to make sure. A huge weight is rolling off me, and I can't quite believe it.

Mom looks at me. "You can't possibly remember this."

"When I was making up that collage for Emma, when she moved out, I looked at all the old photographs." I look up at Mom and start to cry. "The doll's in all the photographs before Emma's accident, and then it's gone. I thought I dropped it in the road. I thought that was why Emma turned back."

She puts her hands up to her mouth. "Oh, Rachel. Oh, honey." Then she lowers them again. "All this time, you've been thinking…Why on earth didn't you say anything?"

"I don't know why I didn't. I guess I didn't want to know for sure." I brush the back of my hand across my eyes. "You know. In case it was my fault."

"Oh, honey," she says. "Oh, honey. Even if you had dropped your doll, it wouldn't have been your fault. You were just a little kid."

She kneels down to hug me, and for a second, I let her. It feels really good. It feels like maybe everything might somehow end up being okay after all. But then I remember Will and the way Mom's been lying to us all, and I pull away.

Twenty-Eight

We eat lunch at a cheap restaurant on the main drag.

"What do you want to do this afternoon?" Mom asks.

I shrug. I don't much care. We're in this weird limbo, and she never did answer my question about how long we're staying here.

"How about new swimsuits then?" she says.

I guess that means we're going to continue with this vacation charade.

Tim takes about thirty seconds to pick out a pair of black swim trunks. He waits for a while as Mom and I browse; then he hands his trunks to Mom and says he's going for a walk.

Mom hesitates. "Don't go too far."

He rolls his eyes, and again I have that realization that he's growing up. He doesn't have a little boy face anymore.

Mom buys herself a navy and turquoise one-piece. I try on about twenty bikinis and finally choose one. It's dark green with white edging and thin white straps. I love it.

"You look gorgeous," Mom tells me.

I turn around, eyeing my reflection in the mirror and wondering if Col will see me in it. I wonder if I'll wear it anywhere other than the hotel pool. It's still January. It's probably snowing back home.

"Do you want it?" she asks.

I nod. "Yeah." In the mirror, I can see her smiling at me, teeth white against her tan. "Mom?"

"Mmm-hmm?"

I never thought I'd feel this way, but I miss Georgetown. I wonder if *Shared Dreams* is back in the water yet, and what Becca is doing, and whether she's told Col that I've gone to Nassau. For most of this trip, I've been desperate to get back to Canada, but now I'm not so sure. It's hard to imagine just sliding back into my old life. "What are we doing now? I mean, are we going to finish this trip? Like, keep sailing together?"

"Oh, Rachel, I don't know." She looks at me. "It wasn't really going so well, was it? Anyway, you were the one that was so upset about leaving Emma and your friends. I'd have thought you'd be pleased to go home sooner."

I turn the bikini in my hands, run my fingers along the white edging. If we have to fly back to Canada now, without even saying good-bye to anyone, it'll feel so wrong. Anyway, our house is rented out to strangers for a year.

I don't know where we'd live. "You said we'd go back to Georgetown. You promised."

"Well, we will."

To see Dad, or to see Will? I don't ask. "When, though?"

She looks irritated. "I don't know. When I'm ready, I guess."

"I don't get why you wanted Tim and me to come with you."

"Why wouldn't I?"

"You wanted to get away to think. Anyway, you took off for the whole morning without even telling us. So obviously you want to be alone."

She folds her swimsuit over her arm and heads toward the counter. "Well, I didn't want to be worrying about you two. I suppose I thought you'd be safer here with me."

"We were safe enough in Georgetown."

"Please. Tim ran off to look for a drunk old man and you..." She breaks off. "How old was that guy you were with? Your dad said..."

"Twenty-five." My cheeks are getting hot. "I know that's older than me, but it's not like there's been anyone around who's my age."

"See, that kind of logic is exactly why I didn't feel comfortable leaving you there."

"What does that mean? You haven't even met Col and you're making these judgments." The girl behind the counter isn't much older than me. Her face is round and sort of shiny, and I can see that she's listening to every word. I lower my voice. "That's not fair, Mom."

"I don't need to meet him," she says. "He's twenty-five. You're sixteen. Doesn't that say it all?"

"No, it says nothing. We're two people, Mom, not just numbers. Not just our ages."

She shakes her head and looks sympathetic, which infuriates me. "Honey, maybe you think you have something special with this guy, but any twenty-five-year-old who's spending his time with a sixteen-year-old is…well, let's just say, his motives might not be exactly pure."

I feel like she's punched me in the stomach. For a moment, I can hardly breathe. *Lots of girls. Lots.*

"It wasn't like that," I say. I look away from Mom and gaze past her at the racks of clothes. Everything is a blur of color. Maybe it was like that. Maybe that's all it was to him. I bite my lip, hard. I don't want to cry.

"Rachel, I want you to be safe and happy. That's all. I don't want to see you taken advantage of. I don't want you to get hurt."

"Col didn't hurt me," I say. "You did."

She looks shocked for about half a second. Then her expression changes to annoyance. "I'm only pointing out what would be obvious to anyone with an adult perspective. Which you don't have. And which a twenty-five-year-old most certainly should."

"That's not what I mean." A cold fury is filling my belly, rising up my throat, pounding in my head. I raise my voice, throwing the words at her like sharp little rocks.

"I mean you and Will. That's what I mean. You screwing around with that asshole Will."

Behind the counter, the girl's eyes are practically popping out.

Mom just stares at me. Her face turns white; then the color rushes back and her cheeks are stained with red. "Will," she says. "That night at the Peace and Plenty, when you were so rude to him...I wondered."

"We saw you," I say. "Tim and me. We saw you with him."

She doesn't say anything right away. Then she shakes her head like she can't believe what I'm suggesting. "Rachel, I don't know what you think you saw, but before you jump to conclusions..."

She's still lying to me. "You were kissing him," I say. "He was naked and had his hands on your ass, okay? I didn't have to jump to anything. It was pretty obvious." I start to cry. "Stop pretending. I hate it. Don't lie to me."

The girl behind the counter is staring openly now, lips slightly parted.

Mom stares at me for a long moment. Then she walks over to her and drops the swimsuits on the counter. "On Visa," she tells the girl. Her voice is as clear and sharp-edged as broken glass.

The girl rings our purchase through without a word. She keeps peeking at me. I bet she can't wait to call her friends and tell them all about it.

Mom and I walk back to the hotel, neither of us saying a word. My mind is racing. Even though I knew the truth, I was hoping she'd deny it. That we could go back to the way things were and pretend it never happened.

We walk up the flight of stairs to our room. Tim's there, sitting on his bed reading a book. He looks up, opens his mouth to ask a question and then shuts it again.

"I guess the three of us need to talk," Mom says. She sits down beside Tim.

I don't sit. I stand there, holding myself tightly. I don't know how I expected her to react. Shocked, I guess, maybe angry. Maybe ashamed or guilty or scared that I'd tell Dad. Not like this. Not like she's done nothing wrong.

"Rachel told me that you saw me with Will," she says to Tim.

His mouth opens slightly, but nothing comes out. Then his face turns a blotchy red, and he looks away.

Mom touches his shoulder lightly; then she folds her hands together in her lap. "Well, I'm very sorry that you two have been upset by this. Obviously I didn't intend for you to find out in the way you did."

"Oh, like there would have been a good way to find out?"

"Rachel…" Mom's voice has that I'm-warning-you tone, but I don't care.

"I guess you could have brought it up at dinner one night," I say. "That would have been nice. Or maybe you could've got Will to announce it on the cruiser's net."

She stands up. "I don't think there's much point in continuing this conversation."

"You don't?" I stare at her. "You don't think you at least owe us some kind of explanation?"

"No, Rachel. I don't think it's appropriate that you even know about it."

I look at Tim, but he doesn't say anything. I dig my nails into my palms. "Maybe you should've thought about that before you made out with him in full view of the whole anchorage."

Mom's face is flushed and her voice is clipped. "That's enough, Rachel. I'm not going to make things worse by discussing it further."

I'm so mad I can hardly think. I walk into the bathroom, slam the door behind me and peel off my clothes. I can hear her saying something, but I don't want to listen. I lock the door and turn on the shower full force. Then I sit on the bathtub floor and cry. She admitted it. It really happened.

The water is so hot, it's almost scalding. My skin turns lobster red, and the bathroom slowly fills with steam. I force myself to sit there and let the noise and heat of the water drown out everything I feel. After a while, I start to feel calmer. I get up and turn off the taps. I dry myself with a big white towel and pull on my shorts and T-shirt. I rub one hand on the fogged-up mirror and peer into the little circle of glass I've cleared. Two blurry, red-rimmed eyes look back at me.

I can't believe she didn't deny it.

Sooner or later, I'm going to have to face her, so I force myself to open the door and walk back into the bedroom. Mom's still sitting on the bed, and she has her arms around Tim. He's crying. I start feeling angry all over again. I want to walk over there and shake her. Him too, for crying and letting her comfort him. Instead I just stand by the bathroom door, watching and feeling like none of this is real.

Finally, Mom looks up at me. She pushes Tim's hair off his forehead. "Well, you okay, Tim?"

Tim rubs his face with his hands. His eyes and cheeks are all red and puffy. "Sorry," he says hoarsely.

Mom's eyes are shiny with tears.

I look at the two of them and feel like I'm going to explode. Tim might be ready to forgive her, but I'm not. "I'm going out," I say. I don't wait for an answer. I just walk out of the room, down the stairs and out into the street. I walk until it's dark. I walk until I feel like I can't take another step. And then I turn around and walk back to the hotel, because I have no money, and I don't know anyone, and I don't know what else to do.

Twenty-Nine

When I get back, Mom's sitting on her bed, leaning against her pillows and sucking on the end of her pen.

She puts her notebook down beside her as I come into the room. "God, Rachel. You've been gone hours. I'm glad you're okay."

I give a short laugh. I am so not okay.

"Can we talk about this?" she says.

"Where's Tim?"

"He went down for a swim." She pats the bed beside her. "Come on. We have to talk."

I stand there with my arms folded across my chest like a shield. "What is there to say? You cheated on Dad. With that loser. God, Mom. If you were going to cheat, couldn't you at least have some taste?"

"That isn't really the point, is it, Rachel? This is about me, not about Will."

"It looked to me like it was about Will."

Mom leans forward, wrapping her arms around

her knees. "I am sorry I hurt you and Tim. I guess that explains your behavior lately."

"I don't think my behavior is what needs explaining," I say stiffly.

"Is that what you want? An explanation?"

"I don't know." I stare down at my feet. My soles are sore from walking so far in sandals, and my ankle has started aching again. "Was it just that kiss or did you actually have an affair?"

"Don't ask me that, Rachel. It's really none of your business. And what difference would it make?"

If it was just a kiss, she would have said so. I wish I hadn't asked. "I won't tell Dad," I say.

She puts her hands against her face, sighs and slides them down so she's just covering her mouth and chin. "Why are you so angry with your father?"

I shrug and don't say anything.

"You were crazy about him when you were younger."

A lot younger. "I know. I've seen the pictures."

"Rachel." She sighs and drops her hands to her lap. "He may not always be so good at showing it, but he does love you. All three of you. It's one of the reasons we're still together."

"I didn't know you were. Anyway, the whole staying-together-for-the-kids thing is overrated if it means we have to listen to you fight all the time."

"I didn't say we'd stayed together *for* you. I said we'd stayed together because we both love you. It's a pretty big thing to have in common."

I don't say anything, and Mom is quiet for a minute. "I know you think you're doing me a favor by saying you won't tell him," she says at last. "But I'm going to tell him myself. I'm not asking you to keep any secrets."

"You'll tell him?" I can't imagine. "What will he…?"

Her voice is bitter. "He's hardly in a position to pass judgment."

I swallow hard. I don't think I want to know what she means. "Mom…"

Mom closes her eyes for a few seconds. When she opens them again, they are wet with tears. She blinks them away and shakes her head slowly. "I shouldn't have said that. I'm sorry. Just forget I said that."

As if I can. I stare at my mother and feel like I don't know her at all. "Mom? What happens now? I mean, you said we'd go back to Georgetown after you'd had time to think, but…" I trail off. "Are you going back to see Dad? Or Will?"

"Oh, honey. Will's not important."

I don't understand this. I don't understand anything about this. My throat aches from trying not to cry. "Why?" I say at last. "If he's not important, then why?"

She gives this big sigh, like I'm asking the wrong questions. Like it's all so complicated, and I'm too young and stupid to understand.

"Is it because of you and Dad fighting?" I ask.

"Oh, honey." She spreads her fingers out, splaying her hands over her knees, and stares at them for a long moment. "It's more complicated than that." She shakes her head, still looking down at her hands. "I wish there was something I could say that would make you feel better."

I stare at her. "I don't want you to make me feel better. I want to know why you did it." My voice comes out louder and angrier than I expect it to.

"Why I did it?" She looks at me and shrugs. "Why do any of us do anything? I don't know Rachel. I don't know why."

I feel like the ground is slipping away. "There has to be some reason," I argue.

"You sound like your father. Always so sure there's a rational explanation for everything."

I stare at her. She's right. "I just want to understand," I say.

Her lips tighten. "I'm not prepared to discuss it with you. I'm sorry you found out about this, Rachel, but that doesn't make it your concern. This is between me and him."

"You and Will?" I can barely say his name.

She shakes her head. "Me and your dad," she says. "We'll talk about it."

"Are you going to split up?"

"I don't know. That's something we'll have to decide together."

I dig my nails into my palms and try to control the wobble in my voice. "How come you get to decide everything anyway? How come Tim and I don't have any say in this? It's our lives too. It's our family."

There's a long silence. Mom beckons to me, but I don't go to her. I just stand there, all stiff and mad and kind of stuck.

She slips off the bed and walks toward me. "Rachel... what do you want? What can I do? How can I fix this?" She reaches out to me again, but I don't move and finally she starts to cry. "Damn it. I'm sorry I hurt you. But I'm not going to let you and Tim slip away from me because of this. I'm not."

I remember the letter that Tim and I found. *Now I feel like Rachel and Tim are slipping away too.* But she's the one who slipped away, not us. I let her put her arms around me, but I don't hug her back. I can't. I'm still too angry. I don't know if I'll ever stop being angry.

Thirty

The next morning, I wake up feeling calmer. Still mad, but that awful anxiety, the buzz and crackle in the marrow of my bones, is silent. Gone. It's like the worst has already happened. Col probably hates me; Mom's going to tell Dad about her affair; my parents might split up. Everything sucks and nothing makes much sense, but at least there are no more secrets churning around inside me.

Since we're stuck here in limbo, Tim persuades Mom to take him to the National Art Gallery. Neither of them expect me to go along. I don't have anything against art; I just don't really get it. Tim can spend half an hour staring at one picture. I think he must see things that I don't. Mom isn't into it like Tim is, but she and Dad have always had a thing about Supporting the Arts. Plus I think she feels bad about dragging us to Nassau and then ignoring us. So when they head out, I stay behind and lounge by the pool. I slather on suntan lotion and stretch out on the deck chair.

It's funny, but we never really lounged around on the boat. We were always busy fixing things, or snorkeling, or doing homework. Neither Tim nor I brought any of our school things to Nassau. Mom doesn't seem to have noticed.

I suppose if we're going back to Canada, there's not much point in finishing up those courses anyway.

"Hey, slacker."

It's Tim. He and Mom are back. I sit up and rub my eyes. I've dozed off in the sun, lying by the pool, and I think I may have got a burn. "How was the gallery?"

"Incredible." Tim bounces on the balls of his feet. "Really, really cool."

"Wow," I say flatly. "How exciting."

Tim misses my sarcasm. "It's in this old mansion that's been restored," he says. "It was worth going just to see the architecture. Did you know that it's over a hundred and forty years old?"

"Nope, can't say I did."

He looks at me reprovingly. "It really was very interesting. You should have come with us."

"Uh-huh." I shade my eyes with my hand and look up at them. "So..."

"I've booked us tickets," Mom says. "We're flying back to Georgetown tomorrow."

The plane lands with a bump and coasts down the runway. Tim and I are sitting together on one side, and Mom is sitting across the aisle. She's holding her notebook, but she's not writing in it. She's looking out the window, and I can't see her face. I wonder how she's feeling.

Tim and I are planning to disappear for a few hours. Obviously, Mom and Dad have to talk. After that, we'll see. Mom says maybe we'll all stay and keep sailing together and try to work things out. If Dad's willing. Or maybe she'll leave, and Tim and I can decide what we want to do. Keep sailing with Dad or fly home with Mom.

I think of Becca and Col and Mango and Terry. All the boats and the clear blue water and the world underneath the surface. Then I think about Jen and all my school friends and weekends at the mall. My bedroom at home. Snowbanks at the sides of our driveway. Emma.

Two different lives.

For most of the last few months I would've happily hopped a flight home if I'd had half a chance. Now I'm not so sure.

The plane rolls to a stop, and we unbuckle our seatbelts. Outside the window, I can see the blue sky of the Exumas. We're back in Georgetown.

Dad's talking to Terry in the boatyard. He breaks off when he sees us coming. "You're back."

We all nod. It feels like we've been gone longer than three nights.

"Well, the boat's back in the water," Dad says. "Good as new."

"Great," Mom says. It sounds hollow to me, but maybe only because I know what is coming.

Dad doesn't seem to notice. "With a little luck, we'll be able to get our old spot back over in Red Shanks."

Right beside *Freebird*. I look at Tim and then at my parents. "Uh, Tim and I are going to take a walk," I say.

We head into town. I feel a little sick, thinking about what Mom has to tell Dad. If Tim and I hadn't seen her with Will, maybe no one would ever have known. Maybe that would have been better, I don't know. It's weird to think about. It makes me wonder how many secrets lie beneath the surface. It makes me wonder how well I know anyone.

I can't imagine what Mom will say or how Dad will react. I remember the words Mom let slip out: *He's hardly in a position to pass judgment.* I think about all Dad's late nights at the office, all those weekends at conferences. If he's had affairs too, I don't want to know.

Tim is scuffling his feet against the sunbaked dirt, stirring up a cloud of reddish dust as he walks.

"I'm never going to cheat on anyone," I say. "And I'll never stay with anyone who cheats on me. If I ever have a serious relationship, there won't be any lies. There won't be any secrets."

"You can't know that. You can't predict what will happen."

I look straight ahead, past Exuma Market and the fruit and vegetable stand, and past a far-off cluster of trees to the point where the road disappears around the bend. I do know it. I know it as surely as I've ever known anything. "It's not a prediction," I tell him. "It's a decision."

Tim's quiet for a minute, and we walk in silence. I try to get my footsteps in sync with his—we used to do that all the time, when we were younger—and I realize that his legs are way longer now. I have to take three steps for every two of his.

He notices and laughs. "Shrimp." Then he sighs. "So, what do you think will happen now?"

I've been thinking about that ever since Mom said she'd booked tickets back to Georgetown. "I don't think Mom would've come back if she didn't want to try. You know? To give things another chance with Dad."

"Me neither. But I don't see why this time would be any different than before."

I agree. But I can't help hoping that they will try again. That they won't give up on each other. That we'll at least finish this trip together, as a family.

I don't know how likely that is. Two feet and ten feet are shades of blues as different as misery and bliss, but when you are floating somewhere in between, it's not so easy to know if you have enough: enough happiness, enough love, enough trust. Our family is far from perfect, but maybe there's still enough there to keep us going. Maybe there's enough water under our keel to keep us afloat.

Anyway, there's not much I can do about it. It'll be their decision, not mine or Tim's. Like Dad says, this is a family, not a democracy.

Thirty-One

Tim goes off to look for Mango. I wander over to the Computer Café, but the computers are down again, so I sit on the curb out front, trying to decide what to do. If I'd been thinking clearly—if I hadn't been in such a hurry to get away from *Shared Dreams*—I'd have brought the hand-held radio. Then I could have called Becca. Or Col.

Col. The sun is hot on my back, but I shiver slightly. Remembering that last night with him makes me feel sort of squirmy. I've been blaming Dad for wrecking everything by calling on the radio, but Col's the one who pushed me away. He's the one who left without saying good-bye. Even before Dad told him my age, he'd acted like we'd been doing something wrong. Maybe he'd already suspected that I wasn't really eighteen.

I'd never admit this to Dad, but I'm actually kind of glad he called and interrupted us.

I'm sort of staring off into space when someone calls my name. It's Becca. She's just walked out of Exuma Market, her arms full of groceries. She walks over to where I'm sitting, puts her bags down and sits beside me.

"You're back! Yay."

I grin and give her a hug. I feel like I haven't seen her for weeks. "I don't know if we're staying," I say. "Mom and Dad aren't getting along so well."

"Oh…" Becca slips off her sunglasses and hangs them on the front of her T-shirt. Her eyes are sympathetic and her mouth is twisted up on one side in the kind of smile that means *ouch, go on, keep talking.*

"I told Mom," I say. "You know. That I knew about Will. And now she's talking to Dad, and I guess…well, I don't know what happens next."

"That's intense." She's quiet for a moment. "I'm glad you told her though. Keeping that kind of secret…well, that kiddie shrink I used to see always said secrets were toxic."

I nod, remembering the awful grinding anxiety. "Yeah. I didn't really mean to tell her, but I'm glad I did."

"I guess even if your Mom stays with your Dad, you guys probably won't stay in Georgetown."

"We won't?"

She shrugs. "Well, Will's here. You know, the cruiser's net and everything. He'd be sort of hard to avoid."

"Yeah." I guess Dad won't be leaping over our table to write down Will's daily words of wisdom anymore. Becca's right. Whatever Mom and Dad decide, it probably won't be to stay here. I hug her again, and she hugs me back, hard. She feels solid and strong, and her black T-shirt is warm from the sun. "I'll miss you," I say.

"I'll miss you too. We'll stay in touch."

I nod, even though I know we probably won't. "Becca? Is Col on his boat, do you know?"

"Uh." She hesitates. "Col left. Yesterday. There was a good weather window, so…"

"He left?"

"Yeah. He said this place was getting a bit too small. He was talking about heading to Cuba."

I picture *Flyer*'s black hull cutting through the waves, her sails white against the water, Col standing at the wheel. There's a lump in my throat, and I don't trust my voice.

Becca touches my arm. "Rach? You can do better."

I swallow and meet her eyes. "Yeah," I say. "I guess so."

Tim and I meet back in front of Exuma Market two hours later. Time to go back to the boat. My stomach feels like something alive is squirming around in it. I don't want to face my parents, especially Dad. I don't want to look at his face and wonder what he really feels about everything.

At the same time, I'm desperate to know what they've decided. Whether we're all staying.

"What will you do?" I ask Tim. "I mean, if Mom flies home?"

"I don't know. I guess you'll go with her?"

I think about it for a moment. "Do you think Dad would want us to stay?"

"Yeah. Probably he would."

It's hard to imagine being on the boat without Mom, but going home now, like this, would feel like giving up. I blow out a long breath. I don't understand my parents at all. In a weird way, it's a relief to give up on trying to make sense of their lives and just think about what I want to do. I look around, at the blue sky and the twisted trees and the brightly painted buildings. It really is kind of amazing here. "I might not want to go home," I tell him at last.

He grins at me. "Good. Otherwise Dad would have given me all the crap jobs."

I guess that means at least three of us are staying.

We arrive back at the boatyard just in time to see *Shared Dreams* being lowered back into the water, her cracked rudder repaired and repainted so smoothly that you'd never know she'd hit the rocks.

Mom and Dad are watching, both wearing baseball caps and sunglasses.

"Hey," I say.

They turn toward us. "Good timing," Mom says. "You can help us anchor."

I hold my breath. My heart feels like it's trying to climb up my throat.

"We're leaving for the Turks and Caicos in a couple of days, weather permitting," Dad says. "We're going to keep sailing south."

I look at Mom. "All of us?"

She nods. "All of us."

There's a long silence. I wonder what they've said to each other and what this decision means. They feel like strangers to me, standing there with all their secrets. At the same time, I have this weird realization that maybe knowing this—knowing that they have these separate lives—means that I know them better now than I ever have.

"Great," I say.

They smile at us. It all feels a bit strange and awkward, like the usual familiarity has been replaced with something new and fragile and cautiously hopeful.

"Where are we going to anchor?" Tim asks. "Are we going back to Red Shanks?"

Mom shakes her head quickly. "No, we'll anchor in Kidd Cove. Much easier for provisioning."

"Closer to town," Dad says. He doesn't look at anyone.

Farther from *Freebird*, I think. Tim and I exchange a glance as we climb aboard.

I take the helm, and we motor out into Kidd Cove. There is almost no wind for once, and the water is smooth and flat and clear as blue glass. I can see starfish and sea cucumbers lying on the sandy bottom. Tim stands up at the bow, ready to lower the anchor.

"Here, do you think?" Dad asks. He's standing behind me and for a brief moment he rests his hand on my shoulder. It feels both warm and heavy. I don't move away.

"Sure," I say. "Tim?"

"Looks good to me," Tim calls back.

I realize that I've brought us more or less to the spot where *Flyer*'s sleek black hull used to sit. For a second, that feels weird. Then I decide it's okay. Col's gone, and we're still here. And at least this way I won't have to look at the empty space.

I put the engine in neutral and then give it a short burst in reverse to bring us to a stop. Tim lowers the anchor, feeding the chain out hand over hand as the boat drifts slowly backward. I rev the engine and the boat pulls back, slow and steady, burying the heavy plough anchor in the sand. Mom stands and watches the shoreline to make sure the anchor isn't dragging.

"We're set," she says. "Perfect."

When Mom and Dad go into town to shop, Tim and I stay behind.

"Buy me some postcards, Mom?" I ask as she steps into the dinghy. "I want to send one to Emma before we go. And Jen too."

She unties the dinghy and sits down across from Dad. "Sure. You want anything else?"

Do I want anything else? Of course I do. But I can manage with things as they are. "No," I say, "I don't need anything else."

Dad starts the outboard and gives us a wave. "See you later."

I watch them flying across the water toward town, the dinghy getting smaller and smaller until it's out of sight behind the other boats. I'm glad Mom and Dad decided to try again, but I don't know how hopeful to feel. I wonder if things can be too damaged to fix. Or maybe they were never right in the first place.

I look around at the brightly colored boats dotting the water, the green hills with their pastel houses, the long white beaches scattered along the shoreline, the water a thousand shades of blue. It's so beautiful that it gives me a funny sort of ache inside. I don't know how to describe it. It's not a bad feeling. It's more like a longing, but I don't know what for.

Tim's gone down below, so I poke my head down the companionway hatch to talk to him. "You want to swim?"

He's piling books on the table in neat stacks. "I want to sort out my books. I'm going to try to meet Mango later to trade some." He picks one up and turns it in his hands. "I don't know when we'll have a chance to get more books, so I should trade all the ones I can bear to part with."

Knowing Tim, there won't be too many.

I hop down into the cabin and take my new bikini out of my still-packed travel bag. Then I step into the head to change. My face looks back at me from the greenish mirror. I wrinkle my nose, squinting at my reflection. I look the same as always.

You can't tell anything about people just from looking.

I climb up on the stern rail and balance for a second, staring down into the water. Before this trip I would've just seen this color as blue. Now I know it's a particular blue: it's the exact shade of water ten feet deep. It's a blue so clear that I can see straight down to the white sand below.

I take a deep breath; then I dive, breaking the glassy surface and plunging through the cool water. I swim down, down, down, until I touch bottom with first hands and then feet. The sand shifts beneath me as I kick off, and I shoot back up to the surface. I float on my back and let the water hold me up while the sun warms my skin.

Blue sky, blue water and hope. Right now, in this moment, it is enough.

Robin Stevenson is the author of five books for children and teens, including the young adult novel, *Out of Order*. She lives in Victoria, British Columbia, with her partner and four-year-old son. More information about Robin is available at www.robinstevenson.com.